I0663614

Swingers

Dick Talent

This Edition: November 2016
ISBN: 978-1-927679-54-8

Contents

Four Play

Contents:

D – Susan Louise Ulga Taylor

My name is Michael Taylor and my wife Susan is an instant slut; just add a good looking guy and she will fuck. This is in direct contrast to how she is in most circumstances. She is a lady to the highest degree, but get her in the right circumstance with the right guy and it is like someone flicked a switch. Gone are every social restraint and inhabitation. Gone are the clothes.

She was surprised by this the most, but I joke with her that it was all in the cards when she married me. You see, her first and middle names are Susan Louise Ulga so when she became a Taylor, that spelled, S.L.U.T.

But I am getting ahead of myself. Let's rewind to the start.

I knew from the first time that I met Susan that she could never get enough attention from men, especially when she was in the mood, which was most of the time. However, she did it all with a certain mount of class, reservation and grace that put her above cheap sluts. Well above. We were constantly doing it and both of us worked at finding new ways to pleasure each other.

I could always tell when she liked a guy; there was a certain change in her mannerism that sent a signal to the guy that told him that he could do anything – within reason - he wanted to her right then and there. That kind of attitude towards sex made me hard and I had to be ready for her desires wherever they led us.

I too am a bit of a charlatan. You wouldn't know it by looking at me or even by getting to know me, but I am an oversexed...well, I don't want to say pervert because that has negative implications... let's just say that I am a man who can't get enough sex, even for a man. I simply love women and in particular, my wife. I adore her, I lust after her, and I wouldn't know what to do without her. So, why I am looking for more then? I am not sure. The story is that one day while at work – and bored out of my mind – I came across a webpage listing all the Swinger Clubs in the area. I was shocked. I had no idea that they were there.

The website eventually led me to a chat line, which after thinking about for a few days, I joined under the name of MT001. I entered as a couple and not as a single man. I told myself that I wasn't here to cheat so I needed to tell everyone that I was part of a couple and that if anything was to happen then she had to be involved. Or at the very least, she had to give her approval, which for the record, would never happen. And if she did, it would make me wonder what she was up to.

At first I wanted to find a woman to join us. Well, that didn't happen. Instead, we went to a swinger's club and well, we sort of just jumped into it. That was a couple of years ago and now we go once or twice a month and try to make an event out of it. Of course, not all nights are good and we've had our share of bad experiences and strikeouts. Those I will leave out of the story because I just want to relive the good stuff. You know the times where I get to play with other woman guilt free as my wife goes off with other men and women.

Back to the present…

As I watched Susan from the bedroom door, I was a little jealous of the meticulous care that she was getting ready because I knew that it wasn't for me that she was getting all dolled up. She stood in front of the mirror checking herself over from her black high heals to her long blonde hair. In be-tween was a little black dress that could only be described as `slutty' as it clung to her svelte body. By the looks of it she wasn't wearing anything else. No bra. No panties.

"You look great," I said and I wasn't lying.

"Do I?" Susan asked unbelievably.

"Yes too good. I am thinking of nailing you right here and now."

That brought a smile to her face.

"I am not joking," I added.

"I know." She smiled. "You always want it. You'll stick it in any warm hole."

"Not true, not any, just most."

After a final check in the mirror, compete with a full spin, she announced that she was ready.

"Wow," I said. "You're a little early tonight."

"Really?"

"A little anxious?"

"Maybe…"

From the way that she pranced to the car I knew that she was in the mood. Part of me wished that it was me that she was lusting for, but the other part was excited by the knowledge that she wanted to fuck a total stranger. She wanted a good piece of new meat inside of her. That is also a turn on.

The swingers' club was in an industrial park and occupied two units of a building set back from the main road. The owners asked that the location remain a secret so that the rightwing nuts wouldn't bug them. I could respect that. I thought that maybe they should go and picket their church on Sunday. Then I realized that, well, no. Most hardcore swingers would still be partying when Sunday morning service began.

Once inside, we got a drink, talked to a couple of friends that we see there all the time and then found a good vantage point to watch the people on the dance floor. This was our routine and it wasn't any different tonight. During so, I saw someone that I thought was from work. He was about average height, was slightly on the heavy side, had short brown hair and was around forty years old. The most distinguishing feature about him was that he had really thick eyebrows. They were like two caterpillars. He was with a woman that I couldn't really see that well who I assumed was his wife. She was shorter and blonde. When he saw me, I knew that we knew each other and it had to be from work. I smiled and nodded. He nervously echoed my actions and I thought that it best to give him so space.

"Let me know when you want to dance," I said to Susan.

"Soon. I want a good song."

Susan and I were on the dance floor and so far we had stayed away from the other couples because we weren't attracted to anyone. Actually, as per usual, it was Susan who wasn't feeling it with anyone. She was very picky and I couldn't blame her. Why would a hot woman want to get it on with some normal looking slob. I on the other hand noticed a number of ladies who I would like to play with. The truth was that the women in these places were always better looking than the men. Actually, now that I think of it, women are much better looking than men everywhere.

Susan liked her men tall and thin. Well, they didn't have to be thin, just not fat. She hated fat. Beards and/or bald were more accepted even though she didn't really care for either. However, she knew that some guys could pull it off. I have seen her with a bald guy and with a bearded man, but never a fat guy. She was picky and quite frankly, she had every right to be.

Finally an acceptable man and his lady made it into Susan's line of sight. I could tell by her change in mannerism so I asked, "So what are you thinking?"

"I am thinking that I want to suck some cock."

"Well alright. Any one's in particular?"

"Yes." She stared right at him and licked her lips.

"Lucky guy."

I saw who she was interested in and again I was a little jealous. He was roughly my height and thin. I guess that he was handsome. She had long black hair and a thin but shapely figure. "Not bad," I said.

"I want to talk to them."

"Sure."

Susan had a habit of when she was talking to a guy that she liked she would ask me to get her a drink. A few months ago, I told her about it and she said, "Really?" And before she could get defensive I laughed and added, "It is actually cute. I mean what are you going to do that we are not there to do? If you kiss him, fine."

"I don't even know that I am doing it."

I laughed.

Now, I wondered if she realized that she was doing it as she had just sent me off again. I didn't mind because Graham's wife was hot and if all went well I would be soon sliding in and out of her little pussy. Linda was one of the rare women that looked better the closer you got to her so when we introduced ourselves to them, I saw how pretty Linda was.

I left them standing at a table and Susan was at one side and Graham and Linda were on the other. When I came back, Graham had worked his way around the table to stand right beside Susan. He had his arm around her.

My first thoughts were: the bastard wants to fuck my wife. Then I realized, of course he does. That is why we are here. I want to fuck his wife.

I handed Susan a drink and I smiled at Linda. She asked me what I did for a living and that sparked a lengthy discussion. I could tell that she was interested in me and that she knew that I found her to be really pretty.

Then she leaned in and said, "It seems that your wife is attracted to my husband."

I looked over and sure enough Susan was sending Graham more than a few signals. One of them was that she was always placing her hand on his forearm.

"You're right," I said. "Are you okay with that?"

"Sure. As long as I get to play with her too."

I smiled. I loved bisexual woman.

"We should dance," Linda said.

"Yep. Let's go."

We walked onto the dance floor and I put my arms around Linda. She looked up and smiled at me and we both started moving to the rhythm of the song. It was some dance crap that I had no idea who it was nor did I care. I didn't come here for the music.

We were joined on my left by Susan and Graham. Linda turned around and backed into me. Her ass rubbed against my crotch and I took this as an invite to touch her. I started with her hips and then I slowly worked my hands up her body, eventually clasping her breasts. She closed her eyes and moaned. I knew that she was thinking of getting to get naked with me.

Susan faced us and smiled at me. I knew that she was in a good place as Graham's hands explored her body. He had one hand clasping her tit while the other one rubbed her crotch. Linda moved towards her and the two ladies slowly rubbed their bodies together. As I pressed against Linda's ass, I looked over Linda's shoulder and saw that their tits were pressed against each other's. Their nipples became taunt as the ladies lusted over each other.

Here we go, I thought.

Sure enough the woman started kissing. To me there is nothing hotter than fondling a woman as she was kissing my wife who is also being felt up. We were four people with only one thing on their mind and the only question was where we were going to fuck.

The ladies broke off their kiss and started talking. I couldn't make out what they were saying nor did I care. All the blood had rushed to my little head and that was rubbing against Linda's nice little ass. I was surprised when Susan started to walk away and Linda grabbed my hand, "Come," she said.

"Okay." The four of us walked to the back and at the counter grabbed towels, condoms and keys. In the main play area we heard the sounds of people having fun. We found an empty locker and started to strip. I had never been crazy about this part as it took out any kind of seduction, but it was part of it. To counter this, I picked a locker that was a little distance away from the other couple and tried not to look at the other woman. Susan and I stripped, put out clothes in our locker and wrapped our towels around us. Graham and Linda did the same.

When they were ready the four of us went in search of an empty bed. Again, Linda grabbed my hand. "Hi," I said.

She giggled and bit her lip. "Hi."

"You look really cute in just a towel."

She smiled.

Susan and Graham led us to an empty bed and jumped on. Their towels came off and they both laid naked waiting for us. Linda threw off her towel and landed on Susan. "Well hello," Linda said, laughing.

I pulled back the curtain because I didn't want anyone else to join us. I turned around to see that Susan was on her back making out with Graham while Susan sucked on her tits. I dropped my towel and admired Linda's naked ass with my hands. Her pussy was very wet. Very nice.

Susan reached down with her right hand and grabbed Graham's rigid cock. Linda worked her way down to Susan's pussy and spread her legs. She ate her while she stuck her ass in the air. Really nice! I slipped on a condom and slowly slid it into her cunt. She moaned.

Graham relocated his cock to the area of Susan's mouth and when she noticed it, she wasted no time sucking it. What a slut, I thought. My god do I love sluts! I am riding a pretty one now as she slurping away on my wife's pussy. As my wife sucks...oh I have to stop thinking of this or I will cum.

Susan stopped sucking so she could concentrate on the orgasm that was about to burst inside of her. Graham moved back, started putting on a condom and we both watched Susan grab the top of Linda's head and arch her back. A long passionate moan followed.

"That's one," I said.

Linda rolled onto her back and as she spread her legs, smiled at me. I wasted no time ramming my cock into her pussy. Nor did Graham because the next time I looked over I saw that he was on top of my wife grinding away.

Linda wrapped her arms and legs around me and I stared at her pretty face. Her eyes were closed and she had that look of someone who was getting off. With each thrust I softly kissed her lips and she moaned. "Oh baby," she said.

I am not sure how I didn't come right then and there. I increased the pace and thought about football and in particular, the Browns. Both Susan and Linda was making more noise as I was thinking about the mistake by the lake and when I was going to see a live game again. Then my thoughts got weird. As I was walking into the door of the stadium I got stuck. "Try again sir," someone said. So I pulled back to try to ram myself in again and each time I did, the doors moaned with pleasure. I tried again and again, going faster and faster until...

I started to cum and I felt all four of Linda's appendages grab ahold of me. My thrusts slowed down but got more intense. I didn't stop until every drop of liquid had squirted from my cock.

I rolled off her and laughed. In the background I could hear Susan and Graham grunting.

"Do you always laugh after sex?" Linda asked.

She rolled over, kissed me on the cheek and then cuddled into me. I put my arm around her.

"You know when the sex is really good that guys think about football or something to prevent them from cumming too soon?"

"Yes…"

"Well…" I told her the story and she thought the image of me trying to ram through a tight door was really funny.

We were laughing as the other two were cumming.

I – Question Period

At work I saw a guy standing in line in the cafeteria with short brown hair and really thick eyebrows and I knew that it was the guy that I spotted at the club on the weekend. I stood behind him. When the guy turned around and saw me, he looked horrified. Yep, he recognized me so now there was no doubt that it was him.

"How is it going?" I said as nonchalantly as I could.

"Fine." The guy's tone reflected that he didn't feel comfortable.

"When you have a minute I wouldn't mind chatting."

"Ah, sure." He knew exactly what it was to be about.

The slow lady in front finally was finished and two other people moved up.

I whispered, "It seems that we both have a little secret that we both want to keep quiet. We should talk. I am Michael by the way."

"Yes. I'm Sean." He looked at his watch. "How about now?"

We grabbed a table in the corner and very quietly he said, "Paula and I had never been in one of those places before. We didn't do anything."

"Sure."

"It is true."

I nodded. "Were you nervous?"

"Yes. And especially when I saw you."

I smiled. "The first rule is that what happens in the club stays in the club."

"That would be good. I am not sure how people around here would react."

"They would be mortified. They couldn't handle it even if we didn't do anything. They would pray for us. That is why..." I made the motion to zip your lips.

For the first time since we had bumped into each other he smiled. "So now what?"

"Do you plan to go back?"

"Yes. I want to."

"And the wife?"

"She will go."

I nodded. "That means she is reluctant."

"Yes." He looked away. It was clear to me that he didn't want to talk about it anymore right now so I said, "Well, if you have any questions, just ask."

"Thanks."

* * * * *

A couple of Fridays later, Sean said that he wanted to meet to talk. What he really wanted was to listen to me talk about the lifestyle. He also mentioned what he really wanted was to find another woman for a three-some.

I said, "The woman are in charge and us men don't mind. We know if we keep our mouths shut and play along then they they we will get laid."

"It is all good," Sean said.

"It is certainly is."

"So what motivated you to allow another man to stick his dick into your wife?"

I nodded. "Are you ready for this?"

"Ah, sure. I think."

"Well, here goes. The problem with most women is that when they are single they have fun with guys that they don't really like that much. When they attach themselves to a guy that they really like, they settle down and become very boring in bed. They trade wild hot nasty sex for intimate cuddly sex. Or in most cases no sex at times, which is far worse. This of course bores the guy after awhile so when a wild woman comes along with the promise of down right nasty fucking, the guy is more than tempted. So by swapping wives for an evening, this gives my wife the chance to be single for a night and go wild."

"Aren't you afraid that the other guy might be better in bed than you?"

"Of course he will be better," I said pausing only enough for my words to sink in, "because he is new and most everything new is exciting and `better' at first. And I don't intend to allow him the opportunity to prove it over the long run. That's my job. I'm the long man."

He chuckled and said, "In more ways than one?"

"I wish." I was confident that I was a good size, but I have seen a few really big dicks in club.

"How did you two get into this?"

"The first time I saw her she wore tight grey slacks, an un-tucked man's shirt and a big wide tie. She looked sexy. One of the first things that she said to me was, `I can't do monogamous relationships. I like sex far too much to be with only just one person.' So I thought, okay, I have a wild fuck buddy. It quickly turned into something more and she settled in and so did the sex a bit, unfortunately. Well, we both tried to keep it new and interesting, but we were running out of ideas."

"Typical for a couple to slow down."

"This made me think about how wild she was before we met so one night we were talking and somehow my wife and I got on the topic of her adventures during her slut phrase. Of course we had been drinking. She was surprised that not only didn't I mind hearing about it, but that I was actually interested in hearing more. I was surprised myself.

I was even more surprised that these stories gave me a boner and not just a semi-hard one, but a fully stiff one. Here I was hearing about how some stranger got my wife drunk, got her into bed and it turned me on!"

"Really?"

"Yeah. I must admit that I am a little jealous, but it is ninety-five percent good. What is perfect is that I get to play with a new woman."

"I am not sure if we will ever do anything. Paula is pretty disinclined. She says that she doesn't need anyone else."

"Most people claim that they would never do that, but when they find themselves in the right situation they not only are doing what they say they would never do, but actually enjoying it."

He nodded. "I guess that I might find out."

"For me it is the seduction that is the best part," I said. "You never know if the other couple will go with it or not until you are actually sliding your cock into her."

"Really? I thought that swingers screwed everyone."

I chuckled. "Hell no. Well some do, but most are pretty selective." I took a drink. "Susan is very selective. Oh my god if the women aren't comfortable with each other then it is a total no-go."

"So the women have to be attracted to each other?"

"No not that, comfortable. They have to…I guess… trust each other. And I tell you, we've had some situations."

"A cat fight?"

"Not that bad, but it is clear when Susan doesn't like another woman. Meow. She will defend her territory."

"I guess that there are some nasty people out there."

"Yes, and some very pushy people as well. There is a part of me that wants to hide my wife away to protect her from all the wolves out there. But there is another part of me that gets turned on about watching her get her rocks off with someone else.

"How about guy on guy? I don't want some hairy fag touching me."

"Don't worry. No guy has ever touched me. All I want from a guy is how he treats women etc. When we first meet a new couple, I need to know if he is a good guy or not. If he is not then it is a no-go. He has to treat my woman well."

"Good."

"Don't worry. If at the random chance that some guy does hit on you, just say no thank you and he will leave you alone."

"And if he doesn't?"

"Then he isn't respecting the lifestyle where the code is to respect what other people are into or not into and not to push then into something that they don't want to do."

C – Mario and Anna

A couple of Saturdays later, we were at the club again having a drink and watching people grind into each other on the dance floor. Rubbing crotches together seemed to be the main focus to-night. At a table just to left of the floor was a good looking couple in their mid-thirties. She was thin and blonde and was in jeans and a white blouse. He was a burly guy in jeans and a white t-shirt.

They would do, I thought. More than do. I would like to rub my dick against her pussy.

"Oh hi," I heard the woman say. The voice be-longed to the woman of another couple as they approached the couple that I was watching. They were also good looking. She was mulatto and he was more or less the same as the first guy. They too were dressed in jeans.

Seems like it is casual night at the club, I thought.

The four of them stood there talking and judging by the way that they were laughing they looked like they all knew each other. The guys were talk-ing and the ladies were standing close to each other. Both of them looked good in their tight jeans and both of them looked really comfortable with each other.

The men left and headed towards the bar and I watched the woman. I admired the way that the jeans fitted them and I couldn't decide who had the nicer ass. I wanted to do a bum to bum comparison.

When the guys came back each one of them handed a drink to the other man's lady. The ladies smiled and took the drinks. It seemed to be the deal closer because after a few minutes, they all started walking to the back.

Oh boy, they are going to fuck.

This turned me on and I wished that I could be part of that. I was actually jealous not to be part of it.

Meanwhile my wife was watching two different couples on the dance floor. The four of them were in the traditional foursome line. The women were in the middle facing and touching each other while the men were behind the woman grinding their crotches into the woman's ass and touching them all over. The only question was if the man behind each lady was her husband or the other woman's husband. This dance usually started off with the woman's husband behind her then at some point they switch. And having been in that kind of line on numerous occasions, I tell you that it is all good. You get to touch anyone you want to.

What is even better is when a good looking couple approaches you out of the blue to introduce themselves. And to my surprise this just happened. I looked up from my drink and saw a pretty good looking couple stop right in front of us. Hello.

"Hi. I'm Mario and this is my wife Anna."

Susan smiled at him, introduced us and stuck out her hand. She usually didn't like Italian guys, but this one met her list. He kissed her hand, which I thought was kind of cheesy. Anyhow, I ignored it because I was far too interested in Anna. She had that classic Italian look and I liked her long dark hair and brown eyes. They suited her roundish cute face. She might have been a little overweight, but I admired the large amount of cleavage that was on display. Nice tits.

For me the best moment is when you realize that the other couple is into you as much as you are into them. As we talked, all four of us knew that we were all going to fuck and that it was just a question of how it was going to start. The women were acting very playful and I knew that my wife wanted to get laid by this guy. It seems that she wanted Italian tonight. I knew that once the ice was broken it would happen very quickly.

Mario was cool as ice, but I could tell that he was chomping at the bit to nail my wife. I know that because I was anxious to fuck his hot wife and I too was playing it cool. And by the way that she kept looking and rubbing against me I knew that I was in.

"Do you guys want to go somewhere?" Mario asked.

I always let Susan handle this question even though I wasn't surprised she said, "Sure, where?"

"How about our place for a drink? We'll just have a drink and talk."

"Sounds good."

When we got to the cars, Mario told me the address, but Anna said, "Why don't I just ride with them? That way they can't get lost."

"Sure," Mario said.

The ladies talked the entire way about everything but sex. I wished that it was about sex, but it was probably just as well because it might have pushed me over the edge. Instead I tuned them out.

Their house was quite the distance from the club so it is probably just as well that Anna came with us. It was a nice two story house on the south end and we pulled into a wide driveway. Susan complimented Anna on the house and the two of them went on about decorating so I tuned them out again. Or was it still? Was I still tuning them out? Probably. Anyhow, all I could think of was Anna's rack and in my mind I had kissed, sucked and played with them in every way at least twice.

As soon as we got in the house, Mario asked, "What do you want to drink?"

"Beer," Susan said.

"Beer is fine," I said.

Anna said, "Are you guys up for a hot tub?"

"Yes," Susan said.

"Good." Anna said, "Then let me show you to the downstairs washroom where you can change."

We followed her down the stairs and into the bathroom. "There are housecoats in there. Put them on and meet us in the kitchen."

Susan and I stripped, put on the housecoats and met Mario in the kitchen. We drank our beers as we waited for Anna.

Mario said to Susan, "Can I kiss you?"

"Sure."

He moved over when she smiled at him. I watched the two of them kiss and I could tell that Susan was really into this guy. Her hands caressed the back of his shoulders.

Anna came back and said, "Well, someone couldn't wait. That's my husband, can't keep his hands off the pretty ones."

At the back of their house was a small enclosed area where the hot tub was located. A single bulb barely lit the area. Mario dropped his housecoat and walked in. Then he helped Anna in and took special care helping Susan get in.

The ladies embraced immediately as I played with my dick under the water. I don't know if Mario did as well, nor do I care. All I cared about was watching the ladies make out. There was no question that they were into each other. The kiss was long and passionate.

After a few minutes I moved to the left side of Anna and I reached down to play with her pussy. However, my hand bumped into another hand. Susan had beaten me there and was busy playing with Anna's pussy. I quickly realized that Anna was returning the favor.

Mario moved in behind Susan and cupped her breasts and nuzzled her neck. I mimicked his moves.

Anna got up and sat on the edge of the hot tub. She smiled at me and opened her legs. Nice. I went to eat her, but she put her hands under my chin and raised my head. She leaned down and kissed me.

"Fuck me," she said.

"Sure."

She reached back and pulled out a condom. I put it on, she spread and when a woman wants to fuck, I don't give her anytime to change her mind. She leaned back and I slid in. Then out and in and out as I watched her jugs bounce with each thrust. There was a lot of flesh moving. Nice.

"Let's get in the water," she said.

I held her and lowered us into the hot water. I tried to be gentle. I've heard that fucking underwater puts a lot of pressure on the woman's pussy. If it hurt her she didn't let on. We fucked like that for five to ten minutes. Unfortunately I don't know what it was, but I couldn't cum. The other two had finished.

"Sit on the edge," Anna told me.

I obeyed. She took off the condom and started sucking my cock. I was certainly hard enough.

"Let us give you something to watch," Mario said. He started to kiss my wife.

I suspected that they overacted on my part, but I didn't care. It was hot and it took me to a good place.

"I'm ready," I said.

"Good. Cum." She said between sucks.

"In your mouth?"

"Yes."

I let it fly and my load flew into Anna's mouth.

When I was finished she leaned over the edge of the hot tub and spat it out. "Sorry, but I don't swallow."

"That's okay," I said.

K – Nerves

At our now regular coffee breaks together Sean asked me, "So how was your weekend?"

"Great. Got laid by an Italian couple in a hot tub."

His mouth dropped open. When he spoke, he said, "I am trying to get Paula to the club in two weeks."

"Good. We'll be there."

"That would be good."

I knew that he had something on his mind so I said, "You have a question."

"So how did you get your wife into it?"

"I asked her, well, how far will you go?"

And she said, "What do you mean? If you are talking having sex with another man, forget it."

"Okay. Would you at least talk to another man?"

"Ah, yes of course."

"Would you dance with another guy?"

"Done that. You've seen me."

"Would you slow dance with him?"

"If you were okay with that. Yeah, sure."

"Would you kiss him? A quick peck?"

"Sure. I do that with friends."

"Okay, lets take it to the next level."

"Would you French kiss him? Make out?"

"Ah..."

"Would you allow him to feel your ass, your breasts?"

"Ah..."

"Would you suck his cock?"

"Ahh..."

"Would you allow him to take off your clothes?"

"Ahh..."

"Would you spread your legs for him?"

"No."

I smiled. "Well, you've done the first few already, now you just have to go through the rest of the list at your speed."

She gave me a look. "Would you like it if I started kissing another guy?"

"Sure, in the right situation."

She thought about it and nodded. "Okay, I can at least do that. I will give that a try."

Back to the present, I said, "So Sean, that was the start and before I knew we were naked with another couple with my dick in some guy's wife as he had his in mine. And all that did it was simple communication and let her go at her own speed."

Sean looked like he needed a cold shower. "Wow. I'll give it a shot."

"Just talk. The trick is not to put her in a situation that makes her feel uncomfortable."

Whatever he said to her, it worked and on Monday we made plans to meet Sean and his wife at the club on Saturday.

I knew that he might be bias, but Sean really thought that his wife was hot. From the brief glimpse that I got of her last time, I knew that she was at least attractive. However, when I met her he was right. She was smoking. She was a short brunette with blue eyes. Her legs were well toned from working out, her ass, small and round, her stomach flat and her breasts out of proportion to her svelte frame. They were big. On top of that she was down to earth and approachable. Add to that a strong desire to fuck and you had the perfect woman. However, this is where the problem started with Sean. It seems that she was lacking in this last category. Well, for now she was. Seeing her, I really wanted to change that.

Nerves are always a big factor and she didn't look comfortable. If she had a desire to fuck, it was buried behind her reluctance to do anything but drink and talk. I asked her to dance, but on the floor she was rigid and kept her distance. It felt like we were at a high school dance. I was the desperate loser who was dancing with a young lady who didn't know the effect that she was having on the boys.

Sean and Susan looked like they were both ready to go, but their stares told me that they were wait-

ing on Paula to made the first move. She didn't and
I didn't feel like pushing it.

After the song, I said, "Drink?"

"Sure."

She seemed relieved. At the bar, Sean said to me,
"How is she?"

"Nervous."

"Oh."

"I think that she isn't ready." He looked disappointed so I added, "maybe next time. She danced with another man and she needs to let that soak in."

"Okay." He didn't seem too happy about. "Susan was ready to go."

"I am sure she is."

"She is smoking hot. Our woman will look good together."

"Yes they would."

We had a couple of drinks and then they left. We stayed.

"Let's go in the back for a quickie," I said to Susan. "At least we can hear other people getting off."

As soon as we got into the locker area, Susan's mouth opened really wide and nothing came out. This was a pleasant surprise. When she closed her mouth she had a big smile on her face and it only took a moment to see why. Standing at the edge of the lockers was a naked black man watching his white wife get changed. His cock was half erect and it was already pretty big. He wasn't that tall, but his body was in good shape. I remember seeing them earlier and Susan never gave him a second look. She normally wasn't into short men and to my knowledge she had never been with an African American. Now, she couldn't stop staring at his long dick.

"Hi," she said to him.

"Oh hi," he said. I swear that I saw his cock jump. "How are you doing pretty lady?"

"Good."

I opened our locker, which was a couple down from their locker and as Susan started taking off her clothes the guy just stood there watching her strip. Susan didn't notice, but the guy's lady certainly did. She rolled her eyes then glared at him. She was blonde with a few extra pounds, attractive, but no beauty queen. Still, I liked the way that her large tits spilled out over the top of the towel that she had wrapped around her. Then she caught me staring at her tits. She didn't roll her eyes, she just smiled.

"I've seen you guys here a few times before," she said to me.

"We come here a couple times a month," I answered, actually managing to look her in the eye.

"I'm Donna and this is my husband Frank the peeping Tom."

I waved instead of shaking his hand. I didn't feel comfortable shaking hands with a naked man with a hard on.

I joked, "We're Susan and Michael and you can figure out who is who."

She laughed and looked at me in the way that a woman does when she is interested in someone. I got the message that she couldn't wait to spread for me. So, with Frank getting all hard over Susan and Donna and I trading lustful looks, it was all the question of Susan.

"We need to find an empty room," Susan said coolly. "Frank. Bring your big dick and follow me."

She walked toward the first room and since the curtain was closed she kept walking. The three of us followed with naked boy right behind Susan and Donna and I walking side by side behind him. I decided that I was going to fuck Donna until told otherwise.

Susan found an empty room. The entire room was taken up by a king size bed. She went in and went to the back left. Frank followed and sat down beside her. Donna went to the back right and I closed the curtains. Susan looked at Donna, smiled then leaned over and kissed Frank. Her hand reached down and touched his big black erection. Donna sat up and kneelt, waiting for me. Her towel fell off and I moved towards her. We kissed for a few minutes and when I looked over, Susan was deep throating this guy. Donna lowered her head and her soft lips were massaging my hard cock.

When I had spotted her on the dance floor earlier, I thought that she was definitely doable. The reason why I didn't pursue her was that I didn't think that Susan would be interested in him. Now, it appeared that she was at least interested in his dick, so what do you think about that; little man and his disproportional big cock. It was freaky in a way. Anyhow, Susan was getting off on it and that is all that mattered.

I watched her suck, lick and jerk his cock. She looked like she was having fun. Actually, I knew that she was. He had a smug look on his face like he knew he had the biggest cock in the world. He wasn't bigger than me, in fact, I think that I was thicker. His cock just looked so much larger against his small body. If he was average height and his cock was as equally proportional as most men's cocks, he would have the nickname of two by four or something. Instead, I named him tripod.

She took one of the condoms from his hand and put it on his cock. He handed the other one to me.

"Thanks."

Susan laid on her back and spread her legs. He slid in without ceremony and she moaned. Donna saw this and mimicked Susan's actions. I was on top of her within seconds and penetrated her wetness.

Frank grunted with each thrust and I thought about changing his nickname to Pit Bull. His grunts got louder as he increased his speed. I suppressed a laugh. Even though I was enjoying Donna's body, but I found it a little distracting listening to Frank's grunting.

"He does that," Donna said quietly. "I actually like it. It is cute."

"Well at least we know that he is enjoying himself."

She giggled.

I had to stop and bite my tongue when Frank climaxed. It was really loud. He stopped, rolled off and dropped onto his back. "That was good," he said.

I knew that Susan hadn't come so I pulled out, went on my back, told Donna to ride me and Susan to sit on my face. They gladly obeyed and Donna set a good pace as her pussy massaged my dick. The friction between our two sexual organs was intense. Meanwhile, Susan's beautiful twat was literally in my face and I was eating her with enthusiasm. Heaven! I was being intimate with two nice pussies at the same time. I found out later that the woman made out while they sat on me - double heaven.

After Susan and I were on our way home we had a really good laugh over Frank's grunting. Or as Susan preferred to call him, Piglet.

Still, it was good. It was all good.

T – Pete and Cindy

What really gets me going is watching a classy good looking woman lose herself in desire. Seeing how she gradually gave in to an object of lust, like a great looking guy or another beautiful woman who had swept her off her feet, then has the orgasm of her life is the ultimate in voyeurism. Passion wins as it consumes her, makes her do things that she won't normally do and not only does she enjoy it, she gets off on it.

And what is even better is when the object that she is making herself all wet over, is you. Or in this case: me. It was pretty clear that Cindy wanted me. In fact, her husband Pete said, "I can tell that my wife is really into you, would you like to slide into her?"

"You bet."

"Then I can fuck your wife, right?"

"Yes."

"Deal."

I felt like I had just bought a used car or something. "Where?"

"Let's let the women decide."

We looked over and they were both locked in deep conversation about who knows what. There was a lot of talking, too much actually. I was getting bored and it was getting close to midnight. I looked at Cindy and she was cute with stringy thin black hair that was cut in sort of an arc around her face. I am sure that the fancy hair saloons have a name for her fancy hair cut, but I didn't know or care what it was. She was a little too thin but that was okay. It was a nice contrast to Donna, the last woman that I had.

Finally they ladies made motions to leave. Susan said, "We're going back to their place."

"Fine."

It was about one by the time we got to their house in the suburbs. It wasn't a big house, but it was homey. Pete took us down to the rec room which had two couches, a recliner and a TV. It was cozy. He gave me a beer and we talked until the ladies finally came back into the room. They were giggling and were wearing only towels.

Finally. Action.

Both woman dropped to their knees on the carpet in front of the TV and started to kiss, passionately. I had never seen Susan be so into kissing another woman before. It was both lustful and affectionate. It was like they were both in love with each other. It was exciting.

Pete took off his shirt and I followed suit. Our pants came off next and by now the ladies were both lying on the carpet. Susan was the bottom as they kissed. This quickly turned into a sixty-nine. There was a lot of licking and moaning and Pete and I felt a little left out. Cindy raised her head and her facial expressions indicated that she was just about to cum. She started to squirm and Susan grabbed her ass to steady her so she continued to lick her pussy. Cindy came within a few seconds of this.

Cindy was about to return the favor, but Pete was between Susan's legs before she recovered. He glided into my wife. Cindy rolled off Susan and lay on her back. I entered her. After a dozen or so good strokes, I said, "Doggie."

I pulled out to let her get down on all fours. She presented me with a good view of a beautiful little ass. I put a hand on each side of her waist and rammed my cock home. I am not the biggest guy in the world, but I am a good size so I was surprised that I was able to squeeze inside of her tight little pussy.

Having Cindy on all fours also allowed Susan to slide under her to eat her out. Cindy was able to use a hand to play with Susan's clit as he ate her. It was a four-way sixty-nine. Hot.

Too hot. I was very close to coming. All I could think of was this cute little ass that I fucking while my wife is eating her delicious pussy while being fucked by and fingered.

Cindy cried out as she came and I filled the condom with a lot of cum.

A – Another Man

Sean told me at our next coffee, "I live my life vicariously through porn. I have been watching a series called Wife Swing and it is blowing my mind. I know that they are only actors, but people really do swap wives for a night like they do on the show. You guys do all the time."

"Yep. I guess that I shouldn't tell you about our weekend then."

"Oh Christ. Did you fuck another woman…again?"

I laughed. "Yep."

Changing the subject, I added, "I have surprise for my wife."

"What?"

"Another man."

"No?"

"The other day I asked if there was any guy she would just drop her clothes and fuck without hesitation and the first guy on the list was Chone. He is an aspiring actor that worked as a waiter at a bar that we sometimes go to. He was black, sorry African American, handsome and looked like he was cut."

"And he is coming over to fuck Susan?"

"Yep. She had her first black guy and wants to try another one."

He looked at me strangely. "What's in it for you?"

"You have never seen your woman get it on with someone else have you? It is something special, but only if you're not the jealous type. Some guys don't want to see it. They just want a piece of ass that isn't their wife. Me, I am the opposite. I love seeing Susan lose control and give in to lust. I love watching her get off. There is a certain glow on her face and besides, I will join in at some point."

Sean shook his head. "I don't think that way at all. I couldn't do it. No way. No way. No Way."

"Well, I do have an arterial motive. You see there is anther woman that I want to join us, so by giving her this, she will be more agreeable to a three-way with a little waitress I know."

"Now, that is what I want: a three-way."

"It is hard to have. We've never had one."

"No. I am shocked."

"You shouldn't be. It is a lot easier to meet a couple."

Sean looked concerned. "I am not sure that I want another man to stick his dick into Paula. It doesn't turn me on."

"Don't forget that your dick will be in another guy's wife or girlfriend."

"Now that turns me on."

"It should."

"Now, what if Paula really loves getting boned by the other guy?"

"Don't worry. She will. If all goes well, she'll have a great orgasm and can't wait to do it again. As an added benefit, your sex life at home will improve. She'll be a lot friskier."

"Well, just being at the club the other night did liven things up at home."

"Good."

"So, you say that I want my wife to have the orgasm of her life with another man."

"Well, at least enjoy it, but don't forget it isn't just him. It is also, you, the other woman and the place. The whole thing is the experience."

He wished me good luck with it and said that he wanted to know the details.

"Yes, I'll tell you all about it on Monday."

"No, email me on Sunday. I can't wait to here about it."

That night, Susan was almost ready when I went into the bedroom. She looked great.

"I have a surprise for you," I told her.

"What is it?"

"We're not going to the club, but a part of the club is coming here."

"How many people are coming over?" She looked worried.

"Only one will be joining us this evening."

"Male or female?"

"Male."

"Really? Who is it?"

"You'll see."

"What is going to happened?"

"Anything that you want to happen and nothing that you don't. You're totally in charge and it is all about your desires. You can talk with him all night or run naked through the streets with him. It is your choice and I will watch. That is my choice."

"Who is coming over?"

"I said that you'll see."

"And I can do anything I want to?"

"Yes."

"Anything?"

"Yes. You can fuck him or get him to rub your feet all night. It is your choice."

There was a knock on the door and I let a good looking man in. He had a seat on the couch and when Susan came into the room, she said, "Chone! How are you?" She had a big smile on her face. I swear that I could see that her pussy got instantly wet.

She sat right beside him on the couch. There was no question that she was in heat. There was also no daylight between them as she talked to him. I placed a beer on the coffee table in front of them and then sat on the chair, waiting to see who was going to make the first move.

As I drank she looked up at him and biting her lip. This gave me a hard on.

She looked over at me with a look on her face that said: I am going to enjoy fucking this guy along with you watching me do so.

Susan admired Chone's tight jeans and t-shirt. The man was in shape and he was handsome. He was also good with people and could walk into a room and take over. God knows he had full control of my living room, including my wife. As he spoke to her he put his arm around her and she snuggled in. She looked up at him, smiling and I started counting down from ten in my head. I knew that by the time I got to one they would be making out. I was right, but way off. By seven he had moved to kiss her and she intercepted it.

So, here I was sitting on the loveseat while a really good looking man was not only making out with my wife, but also grabbing her ass. It didn't surprise me that she had slid her hand under his shirt to feel his six-pack. What did surprise me a little was that I was rock hard. God, watching Susan drunk with lust turned me on.

She tugged at his shirt and started to pull it off. He took it the rest of the way off and tossed it on the floor.

"Oh nice," she said as she ran her hands across his arms and shoulders.

"You're next," he said and grabbed the bottom of her shirt. She reached for the sky and he pulled it off her. She reached back and undid her bra. They started kissing again and he reached up under her bra and squeezed her right tit while her hands resumed exploring his strong arms and shoulders.

I was a little jealous and wished that she lusted after me like that. Hang on, I thought. Yes she does lust after me like that. Howe many mornings have I woke to see that she was either sucking or riding my cock? A lot. She had a habit of getting me hard in my sleep. Is there any wonder why I married her? Is there any wonder that I no longer sleep as much as I should on the weekends?

Now, she had her hand on his bulge.

"Allow me," he said.

He got up and took off his pants. There was a healthy bulge in his underwear. Those came off next.

"Hello," she cried out.

He was a good size, but I don't think as big as me. Still, Susan liked it and she took it all into her mouth.

I moaned because I knew how good one of Susan's blow jobs feels. The woman was a cock sucker and a damn good one at that.

Chone grabbed the top of her head and thrust his hips, making his cock ram in and out of her mouth. He was fucking her mouth and she didn't mind. In fact, it made her job easier. Too easy. He started to moan loudly.

"Stop," I said to Susan.

She pulled her head back and looked at me. "You okay?"

"Oh I am good. It is just that you are going to get a mouthful of cum if you don't stop."

Chone laughed. "That is true. I am close. Damn woman. You are good."

"Thanks."

"Fuck her," I said.

"Will do," he said.

Susan grabbed his hand and walked towards the bedroom. She smiled at me as she walked by.

I walked into the room into time to see Susan take off the last of her clothes and lay on the bed. She was on her back with her legs open. Chone's face buried itself between her legs and by the way he was licking I could tell that he was doing a good job.

I stripped by the door and watched. I was still rock hard and enjoying the show. I liked the way that she put her hands onto the top of her head and wrapped her legs around his back. Her eyes were closed and she was moaning softly.

I went to the dresser and got out a condom.

After she came, I handed it to him and he put it on. She smiled at him as he rammed himself into her. I jerked myself in time with his thrusts.

"Come here," Susan said to me.

I knelt in front of her and my cock found its way into her mouth. She sucked me with the same enthusiasm as she was sucking Chone earlier.

The man could move and his thrusts we rapid and Susan loved it. I was too. Seeing Susan overwhelmed with lust and sucking on my cock like it was going out of style, was too much for me. I came in Susan's mouth and she swallowed me. Nice. She hardly ever did that.

I collapsed on the bed beside them and after the few minutes of feeling the bed bounce, Chone groaned and then the shaking stopped. He was done. I was done and Susan was laughing. "Awesome guys!" She said. "Fucking awesome. Thank you."

L – Surrender

A couple of Saturdays later, we were at the club and I was standing at the bar when the big burly man beside me said to me, "I want to meet your wife."

"You want to eat my wife?" I said wryly.

He laughed. "Yes. I would like that."

I made the introductions and soon Ben and Susan were on the dance floor.

She reached up and rested her arms around his neck in an affectionate way. He was a big one, I thought.

She clinched her eyes shut when his large hands gently grasped her waist. Her body language screamed that she was surrendering to him, he was free to do whatever he wanted to her. And she knew exactly what she wanted him to do to her. Okay, what didn't she want done to her? She wanted to be touched and he was touching her. His hands gently caressed her backside, admiring her firmness and shape. He pressed his body against her small body and she felt excitement roaming in her belly. However, her belly button wasn't the hole that she wanted him to fill. She was silly with excitement. A hard cock was so very close.

All through this, he nuzzled her neck and all the while she soaked up the sensitiveness and moaned.

I know this because Susan told me all this afterwards. To her, it was the all ultimate in being seduced. Every move he made was decisive and she had no choice but to surrender to his advances and couldn't wait until his dick penetrated her. Meanwhile, I seemed to have the same effect on Barbara. My hands were all over her buxom body and she acted like she was having an orgasm as we grinded together. Maybe she was. Maybe I had magic hands. Hmmm…I don't think so, she was just really passionate and go off being touched. Actually, I think that she did because all of a sudden she stopped. She had enough. They thanked us and said that they had to go.

"They're going home to have great sex together," Susan said to me.

"I know."

We were disappointed, but I knew that we sometimes did that so we couldn't complain. That is what they were comfortable with so to each their own, right? After all, this lifestyle is all about letting people be into whatever they are into and not judge.

Fortunately, our disappointment didn't last long. Much to our surprise, we noticed that Sean and Paula had arrived. This was not expected.

E – Parking

We went over to them to say hi. After a while I got Paula onto the dance floor where we picked up where we left off. That meant that Sean and Susan were pawing each other and waiting for Paula and I do something so they could go further. Paula was more relaxed tonight and she allowed her eyes and sometimes her hands to roam over my body. The beautiful woman looked up at me and I saw lust in her eyes. Taking this as an invitation I lowered my head to kiss her. She turned away and said, "Sorry."

I have expected this. "It's okay."

"Let's sit down."

I followed her to a table and the other two followed.

Paula said, "I am not comfortable doing it in public."

"We could always go somewhere else," Susan said.

"Maybe next time."

"Okay."

She turned to Sean. "We should go home now."

"You guys want a ride home?" Sean asked us.

"Sure."

Susan and I climbed into the back and Sean drove. Paula from the passenger seat said, "Maybe we can go for dinner sometime."

"Sure."

Sean drove and before he got onto the road out of the downtown core he turned into the parking lot by the stadium. It was empty. He said, "Before I drop you guys off I think that we should talk."

He parked under a tree where it was pretty dark. Susan and I knew exactly what he was up to and if she did, Paula pretended not to. It turned me on thinking that she wanted to be tricked into this. Well, it turned me on entertaining this line of thought.

Sean turned off the engine and Susan broke the silence when she said, "What restaurant do you have in mind?"

"We like to go to Rocko's. It is our local place."

"Ah, no," Susan said. "Maybe something more neutral."

I added, "And central so none of us have to drive very far."

"Okay, sure," Paula said. "I am sure that we can come up with a place."

Susan said, "Guys can you leave us for a few minutes?"

Sean and I got out and went over to the tree. I leaned against it and stared at the skyline. Sean stood in front of me and looked at me. He was probably horny and frustrated so he wasn't thinking correctly so I said, "Let Susan talk to her and whatever they come up with just go with it."

"But what if...?"

"Hey, do you want your dick wet?"

"Yeah."

"Then let the ladies set the timing and by your not pushing things, will help speed things along."

He sighed. "Okay I guess."

I smiled. "Trust me. It is going to happen, just let it."

"Really?"

"Really. I can see it in Paula's eyes. She wants to, but needs to find her comfort zone. And once she does, look out, instant slut. The two of you will be fucking everything in sight."

He laughed and I added, "Okay, I am stretching the truth a little."

"Right."

"But hey, just let it happened at its own pace."

A few minutes later, the driver's window opened and Paula said. Okay you can come back now."

As we got close to the car, Paula said to Sean, "You're in the back with Susan."

She looked at me and waved me into the front seat. I climbed in and stared at Paula. Susan said, "We talked and we decided to end the night with a heavy make out session. Kissing and petting only."

"Perfect, I thought.

"Remember boys, clothes stay on."

Before the thought barely finished, Paula leaned in and kissed me. This surprised Sean, but he was quickly occupied with Susan.

My hands roamed all over Paula's great body and I couldn't believe that I was making out with someone as beautiful as she was. Yes, Susan is as beautiful, but not too many women in the lifestyle are in their league. Yes, there are some very sexy woman, but very few are as pretty as the two men in this car.

Paula was into it and I could feel that she was losing herself in lust so I reached between her legs and rubbed the front of her pants. She moaned. I continued to rub and she stopped kissing to concentrate on the feeling. She hung onto me and rocked her hips.

"Oh god," she moaned.

I heard similar moans coming from the backseat, but I didn't care. All of my attention was on Paula and her approaching orgasm. I didn't have to wait long. She clutched onto me and buried her face into my chest. Then her entire body started to jerk. She was cumming.

"Oh god yes," I heard her moan from my chest.

"Right there," I heard Susan say.

I looked back and saw that Sean was doing the same thing to my wife and she too loved it.

Paula stopped and remained motionless for a few minutes as we both listened to Susan have an orgasm. I knew that it wasn't the best one she has ever had, but it was still an orgasm.

I kissed the top of Paula's head and she sat upright. She leaned against the window and looked at me. I could tell that she felt guilty. "Thank you," she said weakly.

"Thank you."

"That was good," Sean said.

"Yep," Susan said. "Are you good Paula?"

"Yes." The way that she said was that she was a little uncomfortable so I changed the subject. "Sean do you want me to drive?"

"Ah, no. Let's switch seats."

"Sure."

N– So Close, So Close

"It has gotten to the point where customer service is anything but!" Sean said as a reaction to what had just happened. We were at a burger joint and he had just gotten into a battle with the stupid teenager working behind the counter. I didn't blame him for being angry, but he was overreacting. I knew that something was wrong so I asked him.

"Its Paula," he said. "The sex has been great."

"Oh I can see why you are angry then."

He glared at me. "Funny. She had been all fired up about what happened the other night in the parking lot, but all she wants is me. She doesn't want to take it any further and all I can think about is... Susan. I am frustrated. I just want to do it with her."

"Does she know that?"

"Yes. I keep telling her that we should."

"Pressure. She feels pressured and that isn't good."

"What do I do?"

"Back off completely and concentrate only on her. Don't even mention Susan or me unless she brings it up."

"And that will work?"

"Yes. It might take a while."

I thought back to how guilty Paula looked in the car and I brought that up.

Sean said, "Yes, she feels very guilty about what happened. I told her that she shouldn't because I gave her permission to do so. Still, she is feeling guilty about it."

"Understandable. That should wear off soon."

"Really?"

"Yes. I felt that at first too. We had fucked out first couple and even though I had my wife's permission I still felt like I had cheated on her. She did too. We talked about it and came to the conclusion that society conditions us to feel like we are wrong if we don't do everything the exact way that society tells us to. You must get married, have a certain amount of children and never even look at another person again."

"Yes, that is true. Then why don't I feel guilty?"

"Because you are an insensitive prick that only wants to fuck other woman."

He looked at me and then I laughed. "Just kidding," I added.

"I am not. I don't feel guilty at all."

"Maybe because you haven't gone all the way."

He thought about it. "Maybe. I guess that I should go all the way so I can see if I feel guilty or not."

Then it was my turn to laugh.

T – Four Play

Paula phoned a few weeks later and judging by Susan's mannerisms, I could tell that they were having a good talk. Plans were made involving all four of us getting together and that was good enough for me. Susan got off the phone and said to me, "So, next weekend we're going to Niagara Falls."

"Oh, okay."

"We will share a hotel room with Sean and Paula."

"Sounds great." Hopefully we will share spit as well, I thought.

"Paula is booking a room with two king size beds in it."

My pants tightened. "Sounds really good."

"She says that she is ready."

"Great."

"But I told her that if she has to stop, then all she has to say is stop and we all must obey it."

"Yes dear."

I had all the details that I wanted and I couldn't wait to see Paula again. I didn't tell Susan, but I had jerked off a few times thinking about her.

Since the hotel room was on them, we decided to buy them dinner and took them to a place with a dress code and a fancy wine list - in other words, an expensive place. The women liked the ambience and it set the mood. The expensive wine also helped so by the time we got back to the hotel, all four of us were in a good place.

When the ladies left the elevator, they held hands as they walked down the corridor. They had developed affection for each other and for most of the evening had been touching each other in some way. It was sensual!

Sean opened the door to the room and the ladies walked in still holding hands. They stopped by the end of the first bed and started to kiss. Sean and I walked in, took off our shoes and watched Susan slip the straps of her dress off Paula's shoulders. Her little black dress fell to the floor. Paula returned the favor and the sight of two good looking women making out in their bra and panties made me hard. The bras were next and I motioned to Sean to go in. He moved behind Susan while I moved behind Paula. I pressed my erection against her lovely ass cheeks and put my hands on her waist. Her body language told me that she liked that. I reached up and cupped her great tits. I squeezed. Nice. Very nice.

To my delight, I felt her hand slide between us to find my erection.

"You're ready," she said.

"And so are you," I said.

"Finally," Sean joked.

Paula laughed. "Sean!"

I dropped to my knees and pulled her panties down.

"Michael," she cried. "You're bad."

"Yep. I'm a bad boy."

Naked, she turned to face me. "You certainly are."

I grabbed her with both hands and pulled her close. "I'm going to make love to you."

She smiled. "Okay."

I wasn't sure what was happening with Susan and Sean, nor did I care. I saw that they were on the other bed so I escorted Paula to the nearest bed. She laid down smiling at me. I stripped and she watched. She licked her lips when she saw the size of my cock.

"Oh my," she said.

"I'll take that as a compliment," I said.

"It was, big boy."

I briefly looked over to see Susan sucking Sean's cock. I looked back to Paula and I had a problem. I didn't know where to start. Every place I looked she was beautiful. Her breasts hung down heavily and in perfect shape, her waist was thin, her hips nicely curved and my god, her pussy was flawless. I looked back at her pretty face and leaned in to kiss her.

Yes, I thought. I'll start by kissing her.

As we made out, her hand grabbed my cock and softly massaged it. Nice. I grabbed one of her breasts and cupped it. Nicer. The nicest thing of all was when she broke off the kiss and then dove onto my cock. She took it all into her mouth and sucked it with enthusiasm.

I laid down and as she repositioned herself I grabbed her by the waist and moved her so that we could do a sixty-nine. About midway through the air, she realized what I was doing so when her knees touched the bed, she lowered her perfect pussy onto my face.

I heard the other bed creak and Susan moan, but I was too occupied with the great piece of ass on top of me. Even without touching it, I could tell that she was really wet. My tongue penetrated her hole and she squirmed when it reached her clit. I flicked it as quickly as I could and grabbed ahold of her waist to hold her still. Well, as still as I could hold a woman who was about to have an orgasm. She bucked wildly and I licked her clit just as wildly until she screamed and I felt liquid on my face.

She squirted, I thought. Oh wow.

This really turned me on and in one motion I rolled her off me, got up and grabbed a condom from my pants. I put it on as she waited with her legs spread wide. Very nice. I wiped her cum off my face and got between her legs.

When I slid in I knew that I wasn't going to last long because her blowjob had built up a lot of cum and her wild orgasm had brought me to the edge of letting it all go. I heard Susan moan and Paula was panting with each thrust. Dear god, I thought. I am going to have to cum. No, you can't. Think of football. Fat men banging into each other and grunting like animals. Stupid fat men.

That helped until Paula's panting increased and I felt her soft hands roam over my back. I decided to fuck her as hard and fast as I could until I exploded. This was the best fuck that I had ever had with someone other than my wife. Until now, all of the other experiences seemed to be only foreplay. This was the main event! I rode her like a demon as she hung onto me.

"Yes," she said. "Oh god yes. Faster. Faster."

Of course, I couldn't last and I knew that it was all over. I came and gently collapsed onto Paula. I rested on my elbows so as not to put all my weight on her, but I was close enough to hold my body against hers.

By the silence in the room, I could tell that the other two were also finished.

"God, I feel guilty," Sean said then laughed.

I laughed.

Paula smiled at me. "Thank you."

"Oh, we are not done young lady. That was just the warm up."

"Oh really," she said sweetly.

I looked down into her pretty eyes and as I took in her beauty, I felt my cock start to get hard again. She felt it too and said, "Oh my. You're hard again."

A Swinging Vacation

Contents

Chapter One: Checking In and Checking Out the View

Pay more to get more is what I believe and I wasn't disappointed with the Ocean Front Suite that my wife, Cheri Lyn, and I had just rented for the week in Cancun. It was a five-star resort and I thought that the suite was spectacular with its great view of the ocean.

"Are you happy with it?" I asked her even before the porter had left.

Both the porter and I watched her explore her new surroundings as we waited for her reaction. Well, I was waiting for a reaction; the young man was lost in her beauty.

Cheri Lyn's hair was blonde, straight and her blunt bangs gave her a sultry look. Her thin body looked good in anything and everything she wore. She could have been a model, but chose to be a lawyer instead because she wanted to use the brain that she had been given. We joke that I could never leave her because she would nail my ass in court and if I wanted out of this marriage then I would have to kill her and make it look like an accident.

But leaving her was the furthest thing from my

mind. Beauty and brains, who could ask for more in a woman, not me.

"Well?" I asked. My eyes went to where the porter's eyes were, on her nice round ass.

"It's lovely."

I tipped the porter and he headed for the doorway, even though he looked like he didn't want to leave. He kept asking if there was anything else he could do for us.

You could leave, I thought, but I didn't dare be so rude to actually say it to him. "No, thank you," I said instead. "You have been helpful enough."

She started to unpack and I said, "After a three and half hour flight and an hour ride from the airport, I feel a little slimy so let's change into our bathing suits and took a dip in the ocean."

"Let me unpack first."

One thing about my wife is that she is stubborn. She is going to do what she wants to do and unless you present a strong argument, she won't deviate; such is being married to a lawyer. I have learned to accept this and since I knew that it was probably best to get settled first then I didn't bother to present a strong argument. Another thing about my wife – and probably more of an interest to you - is that she loves cock. I get at least three blowjobs a week whether I want them or not (like any guy would refuse them) and I have noticed when she likes a guy, it wasn't too long before his dick was in her mouth. Yes, we are swingers and have been doing it for a few years now, but we don't do it that often these days and have never done anything while on vacation, even though I have suggested going to Hedonism a few times.

"No," she told me numerous times, "I want to keep our vacations separate from our extra-calicular activities."

Anyhow, we were both here in Mexico - and not Jamaica - to distress from a hectic year and not to chase other couples. According to Cheri Lyn, unpacking was the start of our vacation and everything before and up to that was only part of travelling and not part of the vacation.

The patio of our suite came with a hammock and after a quick dip in the Caribbean Sea I planted myself on it. Cheri Lyn flattened one of the chairs and I settled in the sun! I admired her black bikini as it barely covered her flawless body. My cock liked the view as well because it moved a bit. It was like it was trying to get to her.

I looked out into the Caribbean Sea and let my mind wonder. Every few minutes a boat went by and I watched it. The same went for people and I studied a few of them as they walked by. The majority of them weren't that interesting to look at so my eyes usually went elsewhere. Usually they were pointed at the hot blonde lying in the chair beside me. I admired her soft smooth flesh as the sun shone on her.

A woman's body is a wonderful thing, I thought as I gazed at the way her long legs transformed into a round ass. I stared at the thin piece of fabric that covered the space between her ass cheeks. I resisted the urge to go over, pull back her bikini and rim her. My cock was ready to do its part.

Hmmm, maybe later.

"I could use a drink," she said snapping me out of my lustful daydream. I just noticed that I was hard so I slid my left foot close to my butt so that my leg blocked my boner from view.

"Yes, I'll go for drinks in a minute." When the boner calms down, I thought.

"You don't have to. There is supposed to be a waitress for the beach area."

"Okay, I'll keep a lookout for her."

This distraction helped me lose my boner for the moment, but it soon was brought back to life. Walking along the beach was a good looking couple. She was blonde and a little bustier than Cheri Lyn. Actually as they got closer I noticed that she was a lot bustier than my wife and yet still had slender hips. Her body was strawberry shaped and it was a wonder that her top heavy body didn't cause her to fall over. The guy that she was with was a decent sized guy with a well-toned upper body and a shaved head.

Okay seeing her wasn't helping me lose my erection. Down boy I said to it in my head.

The good looking couple turned and headed towards us. At first I was puzzled by this then it occurred to me that they were headed for the suite next door.

Her tits were even bigger up close. They must be store bought, I thought.

"Hello neighbors," he said to us as they walked past. His accent was southern.

"Hello," I said just before they disappeared into their suite.

My cock was still hard and loved the view around here. A petite dark haired and fairly dark skinned woman came by in a waitress uniform. Her curvy frame and cute face was also pleasing my little guy. "Can I get you a drink?" She asked in pretty good English and her name was Jamie. I know because I read her name tag. It rested there on the upper portion of her left tit.

"Champagne," Cheri Lyn said automatically.

I ordered a beer in Spanish and I watched her walk away. Nice figure, I thought. I pictured her down on all fours eating Cheri Lyn as I took her from behind.

I still had my boner when Jamie came back with our drinks. She was friendly and asked us, "You just arrived?"

"Yes, a few hours ago."

"First time here?"

"Yes at the resort, but not in Mexico."

Cheri Lyn told her how bad the weather was back

home. I barely listened as the two of them spoke. I had a great daydream going on and yes, it had to do with the three of us naked together.

I could go in and masturbate and afterwards take a dip in the water to clean myself, I thought.

"Come," Cheri Lyn said.

"What?" I saw that Jamie was gone and my wife was walking by me into the suite. I followed.

"Close the door."

I did.

She dropped to her knees. "I can always tell when you are covering up a boner and this thing has been up for a long time."

My trunks were lowered and my cock was free.

"Do you like the waitress?" She asked.

"Yes."

"I do too. Picture her and me in a sixty-nine."

"Okay." Her mouth covered my cock and I envisioned my blonde wife licking the pussy of a curvy Mexican woman. Cheri Lyn was on top and I saw her great ass in the face of Jamie. Her brown hands covered Cheri Lyn's white ass and...

I fired my load into my wife's mouth. She swallowed and said, "That was quick."

* * * * *

"They're pretty hot," Cheri Lyn said when we were getting ready for dinner.

"Who, our new neighbors?"

"Yes. We should invite them for drinks."

"Oh, so you would swing with them, then?"

"Hell yes. If that opportunity presented itself. However, I'm not going to go looking for it."

I smiled and started thinking of ways of the making the opportunity present itself.

Chapter Two: The Dance

The view from the main dining room was romantic. Lights shone on the Caribbean Sea and the palm trees moved gently in the breeze underneath the moonlight. It was adding to our distressing. However we still had a ways to go before we were fully back to normal and it had been a long day.

"Oh look, there are our neighbors," Cheri Lyn said halfway through our meal.

I turned and saw that they were seated at the far end of the restaurant. They were seated before I could check out what she was wearing. Part of me wanted to go over to say hello, but the other part of me just wanted to finish dinner and go to sleep, maybe even make love to the wife first.

As we finished, fatigue won and we headed back to our suite, without making contact with our hot neighbors. I held my wife's hand as we walked along the path underneath the palm trees.

"This is a beautiful resort," she said.

"Yes it is, almost as beautiful as you."

She laughed. "Well it seems that someone wants some action tonight."

"Yes I do, but it is still true."

"Can we sit on the patio and have a drink first?"

"Sure."

Forty-five minutes later, we were both naked on the bed. I was between her legs and my barely erect cock was sliding in and out of her pussy. The tenderness was due mostly to fatigue than any love part of it. Well, at least on my end. Cheri Lyn seemed to love the easy fuck. She moaned softly and then I heard her pant quickly.

"Where did that come from?" I asked.

"What?" She was confused.

I heard a woman pant again.

"Listen."

We could hear a woman moan. It was faint, but it was obvious that she was getting royally fucked.

"It is our neighbors," she said.

The image of them fucking affected my cock. I was fully erect, which Cheri Lyn could tell and commented, "Oh that's better. Now give it to me."

With renewed energy I rode my wife quickly as I thought of the nympho next door. I didn't know if she was a nympho or not, but the thought of her loving sex was turning me on.

Cheri Lyn's moans drowned out our neighbors sounds at times. I swear that she was competing to see who could moan the loudest.

"You're faking it," I joked.

"No, just the thought of them fucking is really turning me on."

"Really?"

"Yes, they are both beautiful and I want to fuck them."

I thought of the four of us naked together and I came.

* * * * *

The next morning my wife and I walked into the breakfast dining room. I felt a lot better. We had gotten a good night's sleep and I felt another layer of stress peel off.

In the buffet area we saw our neighbors.

"Good morning," my large breasted neighbor said in a southern accent.

I tried not to stare at her tits. "Looks like a sunny day. Good day to lie on the beach."

"Yes," she said and smiled at me in a way that made me think that she wanted to do more than just lie on a beach. Or was I reading too much into it? I probably was.

All through our breakfast, I hurried to finish. I have never been so anxious to lie on the beach before. We got a few chairs under an umbrella, put on our sunblock and I opened a book to read. Cheri Lyn did the same.

To our disappointment, a large couple from Chicago came and settled into the set of chairs under the umbrella next to us. They were nice but the amount of flab on her reminded me of that awful old joke. How do you find a fat woman's pussy? Answer: flip through the folds until you reach her anus and then go back one.

Awful I know and both the joke and the woman beside me were a sexual deterrent. Sadly the couple from Chicago didn't realize it and they tried to strike up a conversation, but Cheri Lyn pretended that she was out and I kept my nose in the book. I responded politely, but gave no more. The message from me was I'm reading, talk to you later. Still the guy kept talking to us. He tried to engage Cheri Lyn in conversation a few times, but with no luck. Actually, I should say that his penis tried to talk to her and I wondered when the last time he actually saw his penis. Many meals ago I suspect.

My penis was fast asleep through all of this.

An hour later, the hot couple got an umbrella two spots over from us and as they were settling in, Cheri Lyn suggested that we take a dip. Sure anything to get away from the fat couple.

The Caribbean Sea was a little rough today, but I liked it mostly because my wife yelped whenever she was surprised by a big wave. One even knocked her over and she went under. She didn't like it that I laughed at her.

The hot couple came to the edge of the water and I was transfixed by two massive tits. A wave caught me by surprise and it was my turn to go under. I came to the surface and heard Cheri Lyn laughing. "Serves you right, "she said.

I spit the salt water from my mouth. "A little rough

today," I said.

"Yes it is," he said and I saw that they had seen what had just happened. They joined my wife laughing at me. Three to one, I gave up and didn't bother putting up a fight.

We found out that Penny and Richard were from Georgia and had arrived on Wednesday. We made small talk as we battled the incoming waves. I was determined not to go under again so I purposely avoided looking at Penny's rack.

"Where are you eating tonight?" Cheri Lyn asked.

"The steak place," Penny answered. "I think that we are booked in for seven."

"We're at the Japanese restaurant at seven-thirty."

The ladies made plans for the four of us to meet at the disco afterwards.

* * * * *

Just after nine-thirty the four of us met at the disco and for some reason the drinks were arriving faster than we could drink them. I blamed Richard and his constant trips to the bar. The guy could throw them back and none of us could keep up with him.

At first we each danced with our own spouse, but then they girls started to dance more with each other than with Richard and I. Fine, we went to our table and watched.

Cheri Lyn backed into Penny and allowed Penny's arms to caress the sides of her body.

"Hot," Richard said as he finished another beer.

I nodded and noticed that they were getting the attention from the others on the dance floor. It was a nice show until some loud overweight guy decided to get in on it. It took me a minute then I realized that it was the guy from Chicago who sat next to us on the beach today. The ladies told him no, but he didn't get the message. Richard and I were just about to go to get rid of him, when the girls started to head back to the table. End of show.

The fat guy wasn't very popular with anyone right now, especially me.

"Great show," I said to Penny.

"It was fun until that idiot started groping us."

"He was just drunk," Cheri Lyn said.

"I'm drunk and I still know better. Hands off until

you are invited."

Sounds like something that someone in the lifestyle would say, I thought.

A little while later, a song came on which I didn't recognize but Penny said, "That's my favorite song. "Let's dance."

The four of us went to the dance floor and we all danced in a loose square. Cheri Lyn was in front of me, Penny was to my right and Richard was to Cheri Lyn's left. I turned on an angle so I was facing all three of them. Actually, I was facing directly at Richard with a woman on each side.

Cheri Lyn moved closer and Penny copied. I put my arms around both women and Richard did the same. We were now a perfect circle. The women put their hands on each other's waist and smiled at each other. There was chemistry between them.

I wondered how far this would go. All the way I hoped.

I leaned more towards Penny and Richard moved behind Cheri Lyn who leaned back and rested her head against his chest. I followed suit and enjoyed the sensation of a pretty thing resting against me.

I am not sure how they both did it, but somehow they both grinded their pussies on the other woman's thigh. To do this they both had to rely on us guys for support. Both of the ladies' eyes were closed and it was clear that they were both getting off on this.

This is hot, I thought.

I watched Richard and like me, he was careful where he put his hands because this was a vanilla disco and we weren't sure how people would react. If we were in a swinger's club my hands would have been all over Penny's tits and probably would have pulled her dress down by now. Also, I am sure that Cheri Lyn's tits would have been exposed by now.

A few songs later, the women broke it off.

"It is hot," Penny said.

More drinks were ordered and at the table I was just about to suggest that we relocated back at our room when the ladies excused themselves.

The way that Penny walked worried me. She was really drunk. Cheri Lyn was too, but she was still coherent.

"You two are a fun couple," Richard said.

"So are you two."

"You guys like to get a little wild, right? Push the limits." He looked at me trying to measure my reaction.

"Yes. We've had our moments."

"How wild do you guys get?"

I grinned. "Pretty wild. What are you getting at?"

"Can I be frank with you?"

"Sure go ahead."

"Cheri Lyn is beautiful and I would like to fuck her. In exchange you can fuck Penny."

I nodded. "Sure. I would like that, but only if the women are into it."

"I knew that Penny is."

"And I know that Cheri Lyn is too."

The women were gone for quite a while and when they returned Penny didn't look so good. We were quickly informed that Penny had been sick in the washroom. There went any plans for a four way tonight.

Inside my scream was so loud that it would have been heard back home if I had let it out. Damn! Damn! Damn!

Chapter Three – An Interesting Alternative

Richard said goodnight and helped Penny back to their room, leaving us at the bar. We were not alone and two brothers from St. Louis started talking to Cheri Lyn. One in particular caught her eye and judging by the way that Cheri Lyn looked at him; I knew that she liked what she saw. Her body language was saying hey, I like you, let's fuck.

He was a young man of average size and clean cut. I guess that the alcohol was adding to his looks. But then again my wife was sometimes attracted to men that for reasons other than pure looks.

"My brother and I have been down here for a week and I haven't even kissed a girl," he complained to Cheri Lyn.

We were all surprised when Cheri Lyn said, "You can kiss me. I am a girl."

The kiss wasn't long or even open mouthed. Yet it was more than just a kiss hello. It was easy to tell that they both wanted more. I was turned on. My sexy lady wanted sex with a younger man and I wanted to watch. I wondered if that made me a cuckold.

"There at least you have been kissed," she told him.

He smiled. "Yes."

They still had their arms around each other. Cheri Lyn looked at me.

I looked around and saw that the three of us were more or less alone so I nodded. I didn't have to do it to her twice. She looked up and moved her lips towards his. He didn't hesitate and this time nothing was held back. Tongues and lips met and spit was swapped. I heard Cheri Lyn moan. She was ready.

I was too. I had a boner.

After a few minutes they broke it off and my wife pleasantly sighed. "I want to suck your cock," she said, slurring her words.

He half gasped, half laughed. "Sure!"

They looked over to me. "Not here," I said. "Come."

They walked arm and arm as they followed me along the path from the bar to the villas. Thankfully it was dark and no one was out but a few security guards.

"I'm really drunk and horny," I heard my wife say.

We got to the door and as I opened it, they used the time to make-out.

"Come along kids," I said.

They broke it off and followed me into our room.

"You're not sleeping over, okay?" I said to him.

"Okay."

I locked the door and the pair of them walked to the edge of the bed. They didn't waste any time and his hands got busy as they made out. He grabbed her nice round ass with both hands.

She surrendered her weight to his arms and he slowly let her fall back onto the bed.

"Here we go," I mumbled.

If anyone heard me they didn't acknowledge me.

Once on the bed, she wrapped all four of her limbs around him. It was a total surrender.

The straps of her dress were pulled off her shoulders and he pulled down her dress to expose her strapless bra.

She pushed him over and as he lay on his back she went for his pants. "Cock sucking time," she half shouted.

He helped her pull down his pants and she pulled at his underwear. From my vantage point I couldn't tell how big he was because she had it in her mouth so quickly.

He groaned as he laid back and enjoyed probably the best blowjob of his life. He was loud. I took off my shirt and dropped my pants. Then I helped Cheri Lyn out of her dress. She looked great bent over in her underwear with a cock in her mouth. Long legs, a shapely ass barely covered by a pair of white panties and thin back. Beautiful!

I undid her bra and then got on my knees. With both hands I lowered her panties and took in the view. "God, she has a great ass," I thought out loud.

I helped her step out of them and she climbed onto the bed. She made motions to sit on his dick, but I stopped her by saying, "Condom."

"Oh yeah, right." It was clear that she had a hard time thinking right now.

"There is one in my wallet," he said. "It has been there all week."

I retrieved it from his pants and walked towards them.

"I'll do it," she said.

She lowered herself onto his cock and both of them moaned. The passion between them was enormous. It translated into a wild ride by Cheri Lyn.

I dropped my underwear and wanted in so I told her to get onto her back. She leaped off and landed on her back with her legs spread.

"Somebody fuck me!" She said.

They young man beat me to it and was riding her quickly. I moved to put my cock in her face.

"Mmm, another cock," she said. It was the last words that she would say for a while because her mouth was full.

I saw the young man pound away and how much Cheri Lyn loved being the center of attention. Proof was that she hummed as she gave me a hummer. I recognized the tune. It was one that we had made up. The words were, "Two hard cocks. Two hard cocks. See how they cum. See how they cum."

All of a sudden the pleasure stopped. "Switch," Cheri Lyn said. "I want to suck on young dick."

I slid into my wife's very pussy and watched her attack his cock. I wondered how long he would wait before he started bragging about this. Probably will start bragging to anyone who would listen tomorrow, I thought.

Cheri Lyn' small hand caressed his balls and he loved it. With her other hand and mouth she massaged his shaft. She was trying to make him cum.

He did.

It was time for me to release my load too.

Chapter Four – I Did What?

My wife didn't wake up very quickly the next morning. It was after ten when she first groaned and squinted at the alarm clock.

"Good morning," I said brightly.

She glared at me and looked at me strangely on her way to the washroom. "God, did I actually fuck a kid last night?"

"Yep. And for your information, he was twenty-three."

She stopped and cringed. "Oh god. Sorry."

"It was fun. And I was in total control of the situation. No worries."

She peered at me. "You let me fuck another guy?"

"We fucked too. You and I, I mean. It was hot. You were pretty turned on."

"I was drunk."

"Whatever."

"Don't let me do that again please."

"Why? We are on vacation and all three of us had a

good time."

She glared at me. "You only let me do that because you want to fuck Jamie."

I was surprised. "Um, no. I let it happen because it was hot, that's all."

"So you don't want to fuck Jamie then?"

"I do, but that is a separate thing from what happened last night."

* * * * *

At breakfast, which was really around lunch time, we saw Richard and Penny walking in and they weren't moving too quickly. They saw us and I motioned for them to join us. They sat down at our table and Penny immediately said, "I am so sorry about getting so drunk last night."

"No problem."

"No it is not. I ruined our plans for fun last night."

"There is always tonight," Cheri Lyn said. She noticed how drained Penny looked. "Or tomorrow night."

"Sure. We'll see."

"Today we will do nothing but lie on the beach."

"I do like the idea of doing nothing but lying on the beach all day. Maybe I can forget what I did last night."

"Don't worry," Cheri Lyn said to her. "We all have done things that we regret."

Like on cue, the kid from last night and his brother walked into the breakfast area. Cheri Lyn saw him, sighed and looked away. I didn't think that Penny or Richard noticed. I realized then that I didn't even know that young man's name. I was just about to ask Cheri Lyn what it was, but then decided that I didn't care. For some reason I remembered his age. I guess that is what cuckolds do.

* * * * *

Again we were first at the beach and this time we reserved two umbrellas side by side, making sure that no fat people came between us. Things were pretty low key for the morning. I read and the women dozed off in the sun. Richard didn't do either. He laid there looking at the people in the water or at Cheri Lyn. I caught him looking at her a few times and smiled. He caught me checking out Penny a few times as well and gave me the thumbs up. Both women looked a lot better than they felt.

Lunch was brought to us by Jamie.

By the time that dinner came around were all more or less back up to speed. They invited us to have dinner with them. We accepted.

Chapter Five – Dinner Companions

Cheri Lyn wore a white sundress that showed off her tan which emphasized her beauty even more. When Richard saw her, he could barely contain his lust for her. I had the same problem when I saw Penny. She wore a low-cut dress that revealed the tops of two very large portions of female flesh. I had a hard time not looking at them.

We got a table and it was an interesting seating arrangement. Cheri Lyn sat to my left, with Richard across from her and Penny sat opposite of me. This gave me a full frontal of her full frontal, especially when she leaned forward to whisper to Cheri Lyn.

"Again, sorry for being sick last night and not much fun today, especially since we fly home tomorrow," she said and then leaned forward to whisper, "It was a lot of fun dancing with you two last night. I had a lot of fun."

"You seem to be very comfortable with other women," Cheri Lyn whispered back. "Ever been with one?"

Well, that broke the ice in a bull in a China shop kind of way, I thought.

Both Richard and Penny chuckled.

Still leaning forward to give me a great view of her magic mountains, Penny said, "Yes, a few."

"Oh please keep whispering," I said.

Cheri Lyn and Richard laughed and Penny couldn't figure out the joke. That is until Richard said, "Because when you whisper you lean in and give us all a great view of your boobs."

Penny looked at me and licked my lips.

She giggled. "You are a bad boy. What am I going to do with you?"

"Why don't you spank him?" Cheri Lyn said.

Despite talking about everything but sex all through the meal sexual tension built and I knew that for dessert we were all going to have each other.

As we walked from the restaurant nobody said it but we all headed towards our rooms. Cheri Lyn walked with Richard as Penny and I followed closely.

"Do you guys like your room?" Penny asked Cheri Lyn who was directly in front of her.

"Yes, we love it. The sunken living room is a nice touch."

"Oh, you have a suite then. We just have a room."

"Do you want to see it?"

"Sure."

The four of us snickered. We knew what was coming and that would be all four of us naked together. We just didn't know exactly how the seduction was to play out.

I opened the door and let my guests and wife in.

Cheri Lyn locked her arm into Penny's and escorted her thought the suite. Richard followed closely behind. The women discussed the bathroom décor, and then they walked arm in arm down the steps into the living room.

"This is great," Penny said. "We should have paid extra for a suite."

The girls sat on the couch together and I offered to get everyone a drink. Richard helped me and as we were pouring, he whispered, "Are you two into hard or soft swaps?"

"Hard."

He nodded. "Good so are we. Do you have any condoms? If you don't, I could go back to my room to get some."

"No need to. I have plenty. I will bring them out when the time approaches."

He nodded again. "Good."

We both noticed that things had gotten quiet so we turned around to see that, the women were making out.

"Do you think that they still want their drinks?" I asked.

He grinned.

We placed their drinks on the coffee table and sat down on the chairs with our drinks. The show was in full swing. Female lips and tongues were pressed against each other and the ladies held nothing back. The straps to Penny's dress were pushed off her shoulders and the dress flew down below her two massive tits. Cheri Lyn attacked the nipple of her right tit like a starving infant.

"She likes big tits," I whispered to Richard.

"I can see that."

Cheri Lyn put out her hand over her head and held it there. Richard looked confused. I knew what she meant. I went over and hit her hand.

"Tag," I said.

Cheri Lyn jumped up and I took over her tit sucking responsibilities. Oh the things that I do for my wife.

Cheri Lyn dropped her dress and walked over to Richard wearing only her bra and panties.

"Hello," she said to him. She undid her bra and let that fall too.

"And your panties?" He asked.

She shook her head. "Nope. You have to do that."

She bolted out of the room and jumped onto the bed. He followed, taking off his clothes as he went. I too was stripping, which Penny helped.

Cheri Lyn pulled out a few condoms and tossed one to Richard as he approached the bed. "Put this on and take off everything else including your socks." She giggled.

Penny and I made out for the first time and I loved the way that she kissed. There was a lot of passion in her lips. Plus the pressure on my chest from her tits was exciting.

Her hands found my boner and the next thing I knew I was leaning back being sucked off as I watched my wife help another man put a condom onto his erection.

Four horny people helping each other get off, I thought. What a perfect scenario!

Richard slid into my wife and I couldn't believe that he didn't eat her beautiful pussy first. What, no foreplay? Then I came to the conclusion that the entire evening has been foreplay so it was time to get right down to it. I am sure that Cheri Lyn was more than ready.

Penny got up, let her dress fall off completely and walked towards the bed. I followed leaving all of my clothes behind.

To everyone's surprise, including Cheri Lyn, Penny sat on Cheri Lyn's face.

Oh this is too fun, I thought.

I knelt beside her and took in her left boob. I held it in my hand and my mouth and tongue admired soft female flesh?

I felt a hand on my cock and it was Cheri Lyn's small hand. If she wasn't busy enough eating Penny and being fucked by Richard. Busy girl, I thought. Exactly my type.

Penny gently pushed me aside and then leaned down towards Cheri Lyn's pussy. Richard pulled out and said, "Taste Cheri Lyn's juices."

She deep throated her husband's cock that was covered by another woman's scent.

I put on a condom and came behind Penny. Cheri Lyn's tongue was busy licking her slit. Her eyes were closed so I gently slid my cock towards Penny's pussy.

Cheri Lyn felt it and moved her head down and out of the way. I slid in another man's wife. She was tight, but I was able to get in without any difficulty. I assume that my wife's tongue found Penny's sweet spot because Penny's moans were getting louder. She stopped sucking Richard allowing him to continue to fuck my wife.

I squinted as I humped Penny. This is too good, I thought.

A tongue found my balls and I recognized the soft touch.

I pulled out and moved back.

"What is wrong?" Cheri Lyn asked.

"I was so close to cumming."

"That is what we are here for," Richard said jokingly. "Now get back into my wife and fuck until you cum."

I wasn't the only one who laughed. I slid back into Penny and Cheri Lyn must have returned to eating pussy because my balls were left alone. I had mixed feelings about that. I rode Penny hard. She started to jerk and I figured that Cheri Lyn was doing a good job. She bucked wildly and no one had to be told that she was cumming.

"Oh god," she said at the end of it. "So good."

"Let's switch positions," Cheri Lyn said.

Both Richard and I pulled out to let Penny lay on her back with her legs spread before me. It was a nice sight. Cheri Lyn sat on her face and leaned forward to allow Richard to penetrate her. He and I entered the women at the same time. Penny's tongue found Cheri Lyn clit and my wife looked happy. I couldn't wait until she came. I loved watching her get off, especially if someone hot was doing it. Now, two hot people were torturing her with pleasure. It was only a matter of time before she popped.

I was close. I could feel cum building and the pressure was about to be too much. However, I wanted to wait until Cheri Lyn before I unloaded my sperm.

Her eyes were clenched her mouth was agape and her moans were morphing into a pant. "Oh god," she groaned. "Yes. Yes. Yes."

I lost it.

Apparently, Richard did as well at the same time. Cheri Lyn hummed the line from a Beatles song. "Cum together right now over me."

I pulled out and rested against the headrest. Richard pulled out too and sat back, leaving the women lying in a sixty-nine position.

"Oh my," Cheri Lyn said. "That was good."

She rolled off Penny onto her back.

"Well, we fulfilled the eighth or whatever commandment."

Richard and Penny looked confused so I added,

"We loved our neighbor."

"Oh god," Cheri Lyn said on their behalf. "Sorry, my apologies for my husband and his lame joke."

"Do you want that drink now?" I asked Penny.

"Yes." She sat up and her giant boobs hung heavily from her body. I knew that there was going to be a second round soon.

* * * * *

The next day we exchanged numbers and addresses with Richard and Penny at breakfast. One wonders if we will ever see them again. I hoped so, but you will never know. We saw them off and then headed to the beach.

"I wonder who will be taking their room." I blurted out loud. "We couldn't get that lucky again."

My wife peered at me. "You've had your fun. Enough for one vacation."

"Like you didn't have fun, slut."

She playfully flipped the bird at me.

Four hours later I noticed that some new people

were coming in. I crossed my fingers and watched. I was soon disappointed. Very disappointed.

The couple that took Richard and Penny's old room was much older and were not particularly swinger companions. Well, maybe at the old folk home for blind people. Sorry, that was cruel, but you get my point. They were a big no.

Maybe Cheri Lyn was right, I thought. We had our fun for the vacation.

I put my nose in a book and the day passed quickly as we did nothing all day but relax and capture part of the sun.

Dinner was fine and we made love before she drifted off to sleep. I lay awake for a while listening to the waves wash up onto shore.

I was sexually content, but I wanted more. A lot more. Why? I asked myself. I have a beautiful wife who I just nailed and I was allowed to fuck the brains out of a bombshell last night with absolutely no negative feedback form the wife so why did I want more? And more importantly, what could we do that we haven't done already? We've had threesomes with both sexes, numerous foursomes with other couples and since I have no interest in other guys, I leave the bisexual stuff to the women and the other guys who want to do that.

So, what did I want? I thought deeply and the sounds of the waves were the last thing I heard before I drifted off.

In the morning I still heard the sounds of the waves, but it was partially drowned out by people on the beach. The wife was already up and moving around. I looked at her and she was dressed for breakfast.

"I'll get a table then sleepyhead?" She said.

"Sure. I'll be there in a few minutes."

She left and I contemplated jerking off. No. I decided to let the little guy get some rest so I showered and then dressed quickly. I found Cheri Lyn sitting at a table by the window. A few tables away were two good looking couples that were pretty chummy with each other. They acted like we did with Richard and Penny. Swingers can spot other swingers so I knew that the four of them wanted to be intimate with each other, if they hadn't already been. I was happy for them.

They must have arrived last night, I thought. Pretty fast hook-up.

Chapter Six – An Intimate Group

Because it was our last night, we decide to go to the disco because we were hell-bent on partying late until the night. After dinner we went straight to the disco and started drinking. The place wasn't filled yet but we didn't care. This was our last hurrah.

An hour later and several drinks later, the disco filled up and a woman with rich black hair accidently bumped into Cheri Lyn. It was one of the four good looking people that I saw at breakfast this morning. "Sorry," she said.

Judging by her accent she was Irish.

"No worries," Cheri Lyn said and she touched her shoulder in a friendly way.

This sparked something in the other woman who smiled at Cheri Lyn. The women started dancing together and the guy didn't seem to mind.

Nice, I thought.

The other couple from breakfast this morning came onto the dance floor and the women left Cheri Lyn to hug the newly arrived woman. Their men danced with them and I wanted to be part of it. I couldn't tell if Cheri Lyn did or not.

To my delight, Cheri Lyn was invited to dance by the other women so the three of them danced together with the boys not too far away.

Two couples at once would be new, I thought. If it happened. What could I do to make it happen?

The answer was clear. Stay out of the way and let the women arrange it.

Introductions were made and the dark haired woman was Amber and her friend was Mary. Both women were a little thin and pale looking. It was obvious that they had just gotten here. Mary's hair was short and red so this meant that in the group of three women we had a blonde, a brunette and a red head.

Behind Amber with his hands on her thighs was Mary's husband Alan. He and David were both tall thin guys with short brown hair. To me they looked kind of boring, but I could tell that Cheri Lyn thought that they were both hot. David's hands were caressing Mary's stomach and waist in such a manner that he was very familiar with the territory. I am sure that he was. My hands mimicked his on Cheri Lyn.

Amber said to Cheri Lyn," Want to switch?"

"Sure."

They switched positions and my wife backed into Alan and Amber backed into me. Alan's arms wrapped around Cheri Lyn's body and his hands caressed her flat stomach. She closed her eyes and enjoyed the sensation of being touched by a good looking man.

My hands admired Amber's his and waist. Her butt cheeks brushed against my penis.

Yep this girl swings, I thought.

"Girls lets rotate to the right," Mary said.

Without a word, Amber was gone and replaced by Mary. I admired her hips and waist as well.

Cheri Lyn was now being fondled by David who let his hands brush her tits and when she didn't protest he cupped them for a few seconds. Again, no protest from Cheri Lyn.

This to me, meant several things. Most importantly she was into this and I was free to swing. My hands moved from Mary's waist to her stomach and then to her tits. No protest only a soft moan. Amber's tits were also being fondled.

"Okay, rotate back," Mary said.

The scene repeated with me playing with Amber's tits and Cheri Lyn being explored by Alan.

This is great, I thought. Six people headed for one bed?

"Let's get a drink," Mary said.

The three of us guys were sent to the bar for drinks as the women talked at the table. The guys complimented me on having such a beautiful wife and I echoed their responses. I found out that the four of them have been swinging together for a few months and that this was their second trip together. They had adjoining rooms in the main part of the hotel. They were very interested in seeing our suite.

"You mean you want to see Cheri Lyn naked in our suite," I joked.

"Yes we do." Alan said laughing.

David and I laughed along with him.

The women had a similar conversation and my wife had taken the liberty of inviting everyone back to our suite. When they saw it the women made a big fuss and made a few cracks about us being rich Americans.

All the women sat on the couch with my beautiful blonde in the middle. The men found chairs as I got drinks for everyone and the conversation turned to the subject of swinging. We found out that Mary and David were the experienced ones and had seduced Alan and Amber in Spain a few months ago. This vacation was for the purpose of the four of them cutting loose together.

Cheri Lyn said, "We were with another couple two nights ago. We met them here."

"Nice," David said. "So since you guys are pros at this, want to join us?"

Before she could answer Amber's and Mary's hands were on her and their faces were closing in on Cheri Lyn's face. She leaned to the right and met Amber's lips with her own. Then she turned the other way to swap spit with Mary.

By now Cheri Lyn's dress straps had been pulled over her shoulders and her tits were exposed. She went back to kissing Amber.

"Who is going to be the first guy to step to kiss our new friend?" Mary asked.

"Me," David said.

Mary got up and came towards me. "Hi," she said, looking lustfully at me. She knocked back the straps of her dress and let her dress fall.

"Hi," I said back.

She wasn't wearing a bra and her tits were well proportioned to her thin body. Her nipples were very taunt and one of them found their way into my mouth.

David took Mary's spot and made out with Cheri Lyn. This left Alan and Amber to make out beside them. It was a busy chesterfield.

After making out with Mary for a while, she helped me undress and I carried her to the bed. I got out a bunch of condoms and placed them on the night table. The other four were still making out. I pushed Mary onto her back and I removed her panties. She was a natural redhead and I buried my face between her legs with my arms wrapped around a leg. My hands gently pulled back her pussy lips so my tongue could lick as much of the insides of her pussy as possible. She put her hands on the top of my head and rocked her body slowly. It was a competition to see who was enjoying this more.

Unbeknownst to me, the other four stripped and climbed onto the bed. Mary's bucking got more intense and she came.

I reached for a condom and saw that two were missing, but I knew where they were. I am sure that one of them was inside of my wife. I turned and saw that I was correct. My wife was on her back with David between her legs. He was fucking her hard. The other two were also fucking. I slid into "Mary and rode her hard. I sensed that she wanted a fast and furious ride right now. Her smile was conformation.

After an intense few minutes, I let my load fly and it filled the condom that covered my cock that was filled Mary's pussy.

Cheri Lyn was still getting banged by the Irish guy and judging by the expression on her face she loved it.

I smiled. I was sexually content for now. Well, I still have Amber to fuck. My little guy should be awake in a few minutes. I went to make myself a drink.

When I came back I saw that Amber and Mary

were curled up together in a corner of the bed while the other three were at the other end. Cheri Lyn's gorgeous ass was in the air with Alan's hands all over it. He rammed his cock home. Meanwhile David's cock was in her mouth and she looked like she was in her own little world. I have seen her with two guys before, but one of them was always me. This was the first time that I had been a spectator to her getting it on with two other men. It turned me on.

"Oh someone is back," Amber said. She was looking at my cock.

I lay on my back with my cock in the air. She came over and kissed me.

"Hop on," I said to her.

She squatted over me, and slowly let my cock penetrate her. I saw my cock slowly disappear between her lips and I felt the pressure that comes with my cock being squeezed by a very wet pussy.

I half watched Amber bounce up and down on my cock as I kept on eye on my wife. She was lost in lust and it turned me on. Maybe I am a cuckold, I thought. Or maybe I just like to watch.

I turned to Amber and the sight of a pretty Irish

woman riding my cock also turned me on. Maybe this is what orgies are all about, watching and participating.

Mary positioned herself under Cheri Lyn and playing with her pussy. Whatever she was doing, my wife liked because her moans got louder. Mary's body was pretty close to mine so I reached over and slid a finger into her pussy. The way that her body moved told me that she liked what I was doing. It was my turn to have a three-way with two other people.

It was clear to everyone that my wife was having a really good orgasm. In fact, a few people cheered after she was done.

I rolled over as much as I could so that my face could reach between Mary's legs. I pulled her closer so that my tongue touched her lips. She liked that too.

Alan came and retreated from my wife's ass. He leaned against the headrest and looked like he was ready to pass out. Mary decided to help Cheri Lyn suck her husband's cock and after a few minutes she took over entirely. My favourite blonde got up and went over to get herself a drink.

So we were down to four. Amber was still riding me, I was still eating Mary and David was still getting blown, only this time by his wife instead of by my wife.

"Let's change it up," Amber said. She dropped onto her back and David moved into where I had just been that left me to fuck Mary again. This time I took her doggie style. I watched her pretty little ass as I rammed myself into her.

David came quicker than anyone had expected and he pulled out, leaving me on the bed with the two Irish women.

Alan looked like he was asleep and I looked around as I was fucking Mary. I could see that my wife had pulled a blanket over her and looked like she was sleeping on the chesterfield. David was at the bar pouring himself a drink.

Amber seemed to be done as well. She laid on her side and watched us fuck. Her eyes closed a few times and each time they stayed closed longer and longer. Will she fall I asleep before I come or not, I wondered.

I wasn't sure what happened first. I came and my god did it feel good. The second time is always better. For me it is more intense and gratifying. I pulled out and landed on my back.

"What a night," I mumbled as I lay there. It was quiet, almost too quiet.

I propped myself up on one elbow and looked around. Alan was asleep behind me, Amber was asleep by my head and Mary was lying on her back happily sighing. She looked at me and smiled.

"You were great," I whispered. I looked to Amber to see if she was awake. If she was I would have told her that she had been great too, but her breathing told me that she was fast asleep.

I saw that David was enjoying his drink in a chair. He looked content as he watched Cheri Lyn sleep.

I got up and walked into the living room. I noticed that light was coming from the bottom of the curtain. I opened them and saw that it was dawn. The six of us had been fucking all night.

"I'm going for a dip," I said to David. "I'll be right back."

Buck naked I walked out of the suite and looked around. Nobody else was around so I walked onto the beach. The water was cool and refreshing. I went under and enjoyed my last swim before we had to leave this place. Our flight was in a few hours so this was it, one last swim in the Caribbean Sea.

When I resurfaced I treaded water and I looked at our suite. There were five naked people in there all probably asleep and all were sexually satisfied. I knew that I was.

I smiled and thought about the past week. I decided that this certainly has been one swinging vacation! Imagine what would have happened if we had gone to one of the Hedonisms?

Swinging at a Vanilla Resort

Contents:

Chapter One: Alistair and Barbara

I've been attracted to my wife, Anne, since the day I met her nine years ago and I don't think that I have ever failed to get it up with her. Well, there was one time, but I had the flu and I was just plain exhausted so I don't think that really counts.

Anne has long black hair, green eyes, high cheek bones and a body like a fashion model. Her legs are long and shapely, her ass small and perfectly round and her breasts are perky. She doesn't look like an accountant and certainly doesn't act like one. Get a couple of drinks into her and she forgets about everything and has a good time. Needless to say we enjoyed a very good sex life. Well, I think that it is a good sex life and if you had a chance to get it on with someone who looked like Anne, you would think that it was a good sex life too.

She is tall for a woman and I'm a little taller than she is, but where she is thin I'm not. I work out regularly and I like to boast that I can bench press a small car. We both are proud of our appearance, but, of course, neither one of us are totally satisfied with our own looks so we work at it. We belong to the same gym and even work out together on occasion.

We had arrived at the resort yesterday and so far I've been impressed by it. They say that the resort was fully booked, but it didn't feel like it. This was a sign of a good place and I was glad that we spent the extra money to come here.

Most people I know go to the Dominican Republic because it is cheap. They are crammed into mediocre hotels and...well, those places are not for us. We make too much money to go cheap. And besides, the wife loves luxury. She is after all, a fashion model, or at least acts like one. She certainly looks like one.

Finding a good spot on the beach is easier at the more expensive places. After breakfast we found a spot on our own, but close enough to get good beach service. We read until lunch, wondered off for lunch and came back to read again. Around mid-afternoon we decided to go for a swim and swam out to the row of floating chairs and rafts.

"To them," Anne said, indicating the three floating chairs in a circle.

As we climbed aboard we were shocked that two of the chairs were occupied. On one was a man in his early thirties and the other was woman around the same age. He was on the left chair and she was on the right chair.

"Hello," they said with an English accent. I immediately knew that his warm greeting was more for my wife than for me.

We made small talk by talking about where we all were from and what we did for a living etc. I always liked meeting new people here because you get a chance to learn from a person that you wouldn't normally speak to.

Alistair didn't hide the fact that he liked talking to Anne, especially since they were both accountants. That was okay even though I hated listening to their shop talk. Barbara also was an office worker and turned my attention to her.

"Hang on," Anne said. "I'm having a hard time hearing you."

She went into the water and climbed aboard his chair. He helped her and had his arm around her when she sat back. Smooth. Anne didn't seem to mind and I looked at Barbara to try to gage what she thought of it.

"I like your wife," Alistair said to me.

"Oh yeah" I said and put my arm around Barbara.

"I like your wife too."

The four of us laughed and wondered where this was going. I've always been under the impression that Brits were very conservative when it came to sex.

"Well, watch this."

He leaned down to kiss Anne and I was not surprised that she willingly let him kiss her. I heard Barbara giggle. I looked at her and I could tell that she was trying to gage my reaction. The kiss wasn't very long and Alistair looked at me, also trying to gage my reaction.

"Well then, take this," I said and leaned over to kiss Barbara. She eagerly kissed me back and I felt her hand on my chest. We kissed for about the same amount of time and then I leaned back and smiled at my wife who was leaning her head against Alistair's shoulder.

"You two are fun," he said.

He leaned down for another kiss and I did the same. The four of us made out for a while. Barbara's hands were quite busy. She explored my upper body for the first bit of our kiss then her hand felt for hidden treasure under my bathing suit. She found it. I was hard.

"Man,' she said. "I like big cocks."

Anne heard her say that and said, "You'll love it."

I saw that her hand was also exploring for cock. She too looked like she had a good catch.

"Do you two want to take this further?" Alistair asked.

I looked at Anne. She smiled at me and then said, "Hell yes. Your room or ours?"

"We are in room 134."

"Oh we have to swim back," Alistair said.

"It will give you time to lose your boner," Barbara told him. "You guys can't walk through the resort with your big boners."

The four of us swam back to our respective chairs and dried off.

"Are you good with this?" I asked Anne. We have swapped with other couples before and I knew that she was attracted to him so I knew that this was only a formality. It was always good to ask.

"Hell yes."

"Good. It should be fun.

Down the beach we saw Alistair and Barbara dry off and then they headed in land. We followed.

"Ready?" I asked.

"Yes."

We followed them into the elevator and when the door closed the four of us were alone.

The others moved to make out, but stopped when I said, "Stop. Cameras. We can't give these boring vanillas anything on camera."

"Why not?" Barbara asked.

"Um…" I said, but the elevator door opened at our floor before I could answer.

Inside the room the four of us stood in a circle. Anne was to my left and Barbara was to my right. Four horny people in nothing but bathing suits were ready to go.

"Hard or soft swaps?" Alistair said.

"Do you have condoms?" I asked.

"Yes lots."

"Hard of course," Anne said. She smiled at him and winked. She wrapped her arms around him and just before they kissed she said, "Fuck me."

Barbara said, "That sounds like a good idea."

"That thought is worthy of a kiss," I said and then went for it.

It has been a few months since I have laid my hands on another woman and I don't think that I have even touched a bigger pair of tits than what Barbara had. They were soft and natural and part of me wanted to undo her bikini top to set them free, but another part of me didn't want to stop squeezing them.

"Allow me," she said and reached down and undid her top.

The opening was in the front. Silly me.

The top fell to the floor and her tits hung off her body like two softballs. Nice!

Her areolas were dark and large and her nipples were average size. They say that the areolas are a different color from the breasts so that the newborn can see where to go so it acts like a guide to the nipple. I don't know if that is true or not, but I let an areola guide me to one of her nipples. Thanks nature.

She put her head back and rested her hands on my back. As my tongue played with her nipple my hands grabbed her ass. It was a big ass, but it was shapely. I don't mind a big ass on a woman when she had tits of equal proportion. Barbara didn't. Her tits were proportionately a lot bigger than her ass. This I didn't mind.

My hands lowered her bikini bottom and it fell to the floor.

Anne was on her knees and she was sucking on his cock. I couldn't tell how big it was because Anne had it all in her mouth. I thought that I heard Alistair moan something about deep throat. Anyhow, he seemed pleased and I was happy that my wife was making new friends.

Barbara stepped out of her bikini and pulled me over to the bed. She lay down on her back with her legs open. She was clean shaved and usually I prefer a least some hair down there, but I didn't mind. I will do anything for a rack like her rack. Well, almost anything.

I gently parted her lips so my tongue could massage her insides. She liked that and her fingers ran through my hair. "Oh yes," she softly moaned over and over again.

All women loved being eaten and show me a woman who doesn't and I'll show you a woman who doesn't like sex.

I got lost in pleasuring Barbara and how much she enjoyed what I was doing to her. I was wondering when she was going to cum when she arched her back and started to buck. I hung on and my cock jumped a few times at the sight and sounds of a good looking woman getting her rocks off.

"Oh god thank you," she said when she finally stopped. I was released from between her legs and saw that Anne was flat on her back receiving the same treatment.

With a smile on my face and a condom on my dick I slid into Barbara. We both moaned at the feeling. As I humped her I watched her big tits move with each thrust. They really turned me on.

I'm not going to last, I thought.

I tried not to look at them and I was doing okay until I heard Anne cry out as she had an orgasm. I had to stop or cum. I stopped.

"What is wrong?" Barbara asked.

"I almost came."

She smiled. "That is okay sweetie. Fire your load onto my tits."

That did it. I barely got the condom off in time. My load landed on her large mounds of flesh.

As this was happening, Anne crawled over and licked my cum off Barbara's tits.

Watching her eagerly lick it up as she got it doggie style blew my mind. This is hot, I thought as I watched the action.

Before I knew it I was hard and Barbara saw it. "Hit me again big boy," she said.

"Gladly," I said and I rammed my cock home.

For some reason cumming twice so quickly together is awesome. The second time is more intense and I fucked Barbara hard. I looked forward to my second orgasm. This time I was able to ride her harder and longer than the first time.

By now Anne had licked up all of the cum and now

was making out with Barbara. I loved watching girls kiss.

"Pretty hot ladies," Alistair said.

I agreed and continued to fuck another man's wife as he fucked mine. I wanted this to last forever.

I smiled and enjoyed the moment.

Chapter Two: Lee and Ross

The woman at the table near the window wasn't exactly pretty but was far from plain looking; she was a little overweight, being more muscular and big boned than fat. Her short cropped bleached hair showed more dark roots than it should have and to top it off, she dressed very casually. However, there was really something about her that I found exciting. Maybe it was her overall look and mannerism that screamed confidence. Or maybe it was her outgoing fun nature that I found sexy. Whatever the case, I wanted her. And by wanting her I meant crazy hot passionate fucking.

She looked up and smiled at me. She knew that she had been checked out and I was busted. My wife knew too. "You got busted," she said and laughed.

"Thanks, I know."

"The husband is hot," she said. She gave me a look.

"Oh you noticed."

"Unlike you I can check someone out without it being obvious. I surreptitiously look, not gawk, at someone."

"Burn."

"Yep."

For the rest of our breakfast I tried not to stare at the hottie two tables over.

"I'll do them if they're into us," Anne said.

I looked at her. "You're enjoying this aren't you?"

"It is fun. Different. Maybe there is something in the water here." She giggled.

"Maybe."

"After all it is just sex."

"Okay, what has gotten into you?"

"You mean besides a big British penis?"

I snickered. "Yes, besides a big British penis."

She looked serious. "I don't know. It just happened didn't it? We didn't plan anything."

"Some of the best times in life are spontaneous."

"Right. Plans can be too rigid. Anyhow if it happens again with them or someone else then great. Just don't try to force anything, okay?"

"I will do that," I saw her give me a look. "Okay,

I'll just let things happen accordingly."

"Hi," I heard a woman's voice. I looked up to see that it was the woman who I was eyeing and her husband.

"Hi," I said.

"Can we ask you a question?" Her accent was southern United States. I love a Southern Bell. This made me like her even more.

"Sure." I motioned for them to sit.

They did. He sat to Anne's right and she sat to my left.

"I'm Lee," she said, "And this is my husband Ross."

"Anne and Richard," I said, leaving it up to them who was who.

"Anne," he said looking at my wife. "I never would have taken you for an Anne."

She was amused. "Why? What does an Anne look like?"

"I don't know. I've never met a woman named Anne before."

"Really?" She laughed.

"Never? You've never known named Anne before?"

"How do you spell it: A...N...D?"

She rolled her eyes and laughed, "No silly."

"Well, if Andy is A...N...D...Y, why shouldn't Anne be spelled, A...N...D?"

"Um..." Anne could only smile and shake her head at him.

As they spoke I asked Lee, "When did you two arrive?"

"Last night," she said. "We were supposed to go to Jamaica, but we had to change hotels at the last minute because of the hurricane."

"Oh right. We were worried about that too."

"We were supposed to go to Hedonism."

"Really?" I felt my penis come to life and say, "Hello?"

"We've never been before. Have you?"

"No."

"Do you think that you two would ever go?"

I shrugged. "Never say never."

She nodded and I added, "But you don't have to go there to have fun."

Her face brightened and she licked her lips.

"What are you two up to today?"

"Beach. We have our chair already marked with our stuff." I pointed to it. "Find us."

"Okay. We'll change and see you at the beach."

We both turned and Anne and Ross stopped their conversation. "Continue it on the beach," she said to her husband. "Let's get changed as quickly as we can. Our new friends are saving a spot on the beach."

They got up and he said, "See you two in a few minutes."

After they were out of earshot Anne asked, "What were you two talking about?"

"They were supposed to go to Hedonism."

"Oh boy, here we go again."

From that point it was only a question of when the four of us were going to get naked together. I looked forward to fucking that cute little Southern Bell.

On the way out of the buffet restaurant Anne used the toilet and I bumped into Alistair and Barbara who said that they would talk to us later as they were on their way to an all-day excursion.

"Where are they going?" Anne asked me.

"Something about a boat tour."

Great that left all day to flirt with the new couple.

I saw Lee and Ross coming up the beach and I admired her curves and the white bikini she was wearing. His trunks were tight and I could see which side he dressed himself on and what was good for me was that I could see her camel toes. Nice.

Anne said quietly to me, "Oh my, they aren't shy are they?"

"Well, they were on their way to Hedonism."

"So it looks like Hedonism has come to us."

"Hello," Ross said. Both of them were smiling at

us.

I got them settled in beside us and as we talked I could feel the sexual tension between us. This was added to when Lee took off her top to sunbath topless. She had nice tits.

"If this was Hedonism I would be naked right now," she announced.

"And I would be on top of you," I added, surprising myself.

Ross cheered and said, "Now it is a party."

Lee looked up and smiled at me. "Your room or ours?"

I looked at Anne who said, "Can we at least get some sun and have a swim first?"

Lee nodded. "Maybe after lunch then."

The rest of the morning was filled with sun tanning, swimming and the odd sexual retort. Needless to say, the sexual tension was high and we all rush through lunch. Their room was basically the same as our room and fortunately the maid had already cleaned it so we wouldn't be interrupted. Anyhow Ross put the `do not disturb' sign on the door.

Ross said, "You three get started. I want to watch for a bit."

Lee took off her bikini and laid on the bed. Anne did the same and climbed on top of her. They kissed and I stood there slowly jerking myself off.

"Go on get in there," Ross told me.

I knelt on the bed and slid my dick between their faces. Instantly two pairs of lips were on it. I moaned as both women eagerly sucked my cock.

Ross put his face to Anne's ass and from what I could tell, he was rimming her. Whatever he was doing Anne liked it or at least didn't seem to mind.

All I could think was and blurted out, "Now it is a party."

We remained in this position until Ross announced, "Anne roll over baby." He put on a condom.

She did and as a bonus she spread her legs. He slid in and I licked my lips as I saw Lee naked up close for the first time. Her body was best described as sexy rude. There was nothing subtle about her body parts. Her nipples were large and pointed right at me and her pussy was clean shaven for easy access. I could clearly see that it was a well worked in pussy.

I kissed her first and let my hands admire her tits. After a few minutes she said, "Fuck me."

Guess what I did?

She was tighter than Barbara.

Chapter Three: Six for Sex

A couple of months ago, Anne and I had our first orgy and we haven't repeated it since. In fact, Alistair and Barbara were our first couple since that magical night.

"So who did you like better? I asked Anne. "Alistair and Barbara or Lee and Ross?"

She peered at me and then laughed. "Not sure. Might have to do a side by side comparison."

"Oh that sounds like fun." The more that I thought of it the more that I liked the idea of all six of us together. "I could ask Alistair and Ross if they are up for a six-way."

"I think that would be a sextuplet."

"Nice."

After dinner Anne and I went to the patio bar and hoped that the other two couples would join us there. Alistair and Barbara were already at a table and invited us to sit with them. After hearing about their all-day excursion, Anne said, "We have a confession to make."

"Oh, what is it honey?"

"We cheated on you," she said then giggled.

"Oh," Barbara said and then laughed, "We are so hurt."

Alistair added, "Oh Christ, now you've done it."

Barbara looked at me and shook her head. "You've been a bad boy."

"Yes I have and I want to be badder. I have a plan."

"Go on."

"I would like all six of us to get together."

The British couple looked at each other and he said, "sure, but we have to meet them first to see if we like them and…"

"If they like us," Barbara added.

I glanced down at the cleavage that was pouring out of her black dress. "Oh, he will like you," I told her.

A drink later, Ross and Lee walked to the bar and Anne pointed them out to the British couple.

"Oh we've been eyeing them," Alistair said.

Taking that as a cue I went up to the bar where

Ross and Lee were and asked them to join us. They did and I made the appropriate introductions. It was quite apparent that the southern couple was attracted to the British couple and vice-versa. During small talk between them Lee said, "We were supposed to go to Hedonism," and that really broke the ice. Anne confessed that we had swung with both couple and that we wanted to have a six-way.

"Sounds like fun," Lee said. "I'm in."

A few minutes later five horny people followed me into our room and Anne and Barbara sat on the bed beside each other. Their thighs were touching. Ross stood by the door, Lee sat on the chair and Alistair leaned against the dresser not far from her. We all looked at each other until Anne said, "We should play spin the bottle."

I took a beer from the fridge and put it on the bed between the two sexy women.

"You first," Barbara told Anne. "Your idea."

Anxious to get things going she spun the bottle on the floor. It pointed towards Alistair who wasted no time in coming over for a kiss. It didn't last that long, but it raised the sexual tension in the room.

Barbara spun and got Ross.

"Oh," she said with a smile. "I haven't kissed you before."

She jumped off the bed to meet him halfway. Their kiss was a lot longer. Halfway though it Lee got bored and went up to Alistair. "Hi," she said.

"Hi back."

"Kiss me."

"It isn't our turn."

"Who cares? Kiss me."

He did and I looked at Anne while the other two couples were busy making out.

"Kiss me," she said.

"I can't kiss my own wife," I joked.

I went over to the bed and kissed my wife. There was a lot of passion in it and I had forgotten how much I enjoyed her. Here I was busy fucking other men's wives and ignoring the great piece of ass right under my nose.

Things progressed as Ross and Barbara fucked on

the bed and Lee was sucking Alistair off by the dresser. I had Anne on all fours as I fucked her. We both watched the action in room and enjoyed the show.

Then things go a lot more intense. Anne moved forward so she could kiss Ross as Barbara sucked her tits and Lee somehow got around Barbara to lick Anne's pussy as Alistair shoved his big cock inside of her. This was now truly a six-way. All couples were touching each other and people were being pleasured without exactly knowing who was doing it.

After a few minutes Alistair and I switched positions and I don't think that Lee knew who was now fucking her. Anne came violently all over Alistair's cock (well, all over the condom he was wearing) and acted like she wanted more; a lot more.

What a horny horny slut, I thought. Not to be out done, Lee wrapped her legs around me and matched my thrusts. She too loved being fucked. Barbara and Ross shifted to the doggie position so she could make out with Anne.

Aw, girls are kissing, I thought, isn't that sweet.

It was all too much for me and I came.

For the next few minutes I sat in the chair and watched the action on my bed. Five people went crazy; their limbs touching anything and everything they could reach. It was hot. Ross lost his load next, followed by Alistair. However, the women kept going and I admired them for their endurance. A woman could go as long as she wanted to. What happened next blew my mind.

All three women made a circle by lying on their right sides. Anne's face was between Lee's legs, Lee's face was between Barbara's legs and Anne was being serviced by Barbara.

It made me hard again, but I didn't want to interrupt what looked like the most beautiful sight that I had ever seen.

I slowly jacked off watching the woman. When the other two guys got hard again they joined me. All three of us waited for the women to finish. Lee came first and as soon as Anne's head emerged from between her legs, Ross rammed his cock into his wife.

I nodded. It was a good way to finish. Alistair and I waited for our respectful wives to orgasm before we took them. Barbara and Anne were now in a sixty-nine with Anne on top.

Nice.

Anne jerked and I could tell that she was staring to cum, but she still was able to pleasure Barbara. Before Anne finished her orgasm Barbara started her orgasm.

"Not a moment too soon," Alistair said and grabbed his wife. He rammed his big cock into her.

I did the same to Anne. God finally, I thought.

Anne wrapped all four of her limbs around me as I rode her hard.

By now Lee and Ross had finished and were watching us with a smile on their faces.

I looked down to see how beautiful my wife looked and kissed her. She dug her nails into my back as she had another orgasm.

I came with her and I didn't stop until she came. Then I rolled off her and went into a bit of a post-cumming coma.

I heard Ross joke, "No snoring."

Alistair finished at some point and apparently I had drifted off. When I woke the others had raided the fridge and were sitting around laughing.

"Here," Alistair said handing me a beer. "Let me buy you a drink."

"Ah, thanks."

"So when is round two?" Lee asked.

"Why tomorrow night of course," Barbara said.

I smiled. "Sounds good to me."

Anne looked at Barbara. "So your room next time?"

"Sure, we'll meet after dinner."

I took a sip of beer and never felt so good in my life. Who would have thought that a swinger's paradise could be found at a vanilla resort?

Undercover Swingers Part 1: Five is a Party

Swinging at a sex club is easy, everyone there knows about the lifestyle so it is easy to be free and make-out with someone else's wife on the dance floor; so no one will look critically at you there. What isn't easy is to swing in the vanilla world where people are judgmental and aren't open to adult playtime. Heck, I've heard that a friend of a friend had gotten rebuked in a vanilla bar by a sour-faced woman because he had gotten too chummy with someone else's wife as his wife flirted with the other guy. The sour-faced woman told them that what they were doing was against the rules.

"What rules?" He asked.

"Why god's rules of course," the sour-faced woman told him arrogantly. She seemed surprised that he didn't know that.

My friend's friend and his party tried to ignore this woman, but she harassed him for the rest of the evening. Finally, they had to leave the bar and go somewhere else. However, the woman followed them and continued to rebuke them. Finally, they were forced to go back to their condo. The woman tried to follow them and even followed them to the condo's entrance.

"You don't live here so you can't get in," he told her.

She didn't like that and said so, "God gives me the right to go wherever sinners are sinning so I can teach the word of god."

He had enough of her and her power trip. "Here is my word, fuck off!" He shouted in her face.

"What kill-joy," he apparently said to my friend at the end of the story.

I don't know if this story was true or not, but my dealings if the religious right have been similar; albeit not as extreme; not nearly as extreme in fact. However, their judgements and comments are irritating and I wish to avoid them. Even the looks of disapproval bug me. People can be jerks.

Anyhow, because of people like her I find it exciting to meet another swinging couple for drinks in a normal bar. There is a certain risk to it all and my wife, Monica, likes the whole undercover sinner's thing. It makes her feel that she was cheating the system.

Both of couldn't wait until Saturday where we were to meet a swinging couple at a vanilla bar. It should be hot.

* * * * *

Lea was lovely. She was pretty and curvy. She had nice hips and big tits, which were out on display the night we met her and her husband, Mark, at the club last week. The woman had cleavage and I wanted to fuck her brains out the first time we had danced. Unfortunately, Monica didn't want to do anything with them that night. We had been out of the game for over a year and a half and it was too much too soon for her. For me it wasn't too much, but I could understand that. Having a stranger grab her perfect ass in public took a little getting used to; or in this case, re-getting used to.

Anyhow, Monica agreed to meet them for drinks with the possibility that it would lead to sex. Of course I hoped that it did. I wanted Lea and more than once I imagined my hard cock shoving her pussy lips apart as I gazed at her pretty face and big tits. Just thinking about her attributes made me hard.

I tried not to picture Lea naked as Monica and I walked into the bar. I was already anxious enough so I didn't need pressure from the little guy to hurry things up.

I reminded myself that the women were in charge and set the pace.

Lea and Mark were waiting in a booth for us. As we approached, they stood up. She wore a low-cut red dress and from what I could tell no bra. I could see her nipples indent the fabric of the dress. This did not help me lose my erection.

"You look great," I told her as she hugged me. I whimpered as her large tits pressed against me.

"Nice to see you too," she said while smiling at me. There was no doubt that she felt my erection.

Monica sat beside Mark and I sat beside Lea. Nice. Lea rested her hand on my leg. Very nice.

I knew that there wasn't a chance of my erection going away anytime soon so I decided to just go with it. "The Spread Eagle is where the woman has an orgasm so powerful that she finds it so liberating that from that point on she will do anything," I said.

"Oh," Lea said, licking her lips. "How do you make a woman have an orgasm so powerful?"

"I can't explain it; I would have to show you."

"Of course," Monica said, rolling her eyes.

Mark said, "You know no one in this bar knows who is married to whom."

"Well, the waitress saw us walk in together so she knows that we are together," Monica told him.

I looked across the room at our waitress. She was in her late twenties, early thirties and she was hot. She was young, curvy and pretty; three things that I like in a woman.

She came over and said brightly, "Hi I'm Stephanie, what do you want to drink?" She looked at Monica and me.

We noticed that our new friends were drinking red wine so we both ordered a glass of the same.

"On second thought," I added, "Bring a bottle instead. I am sure that it won't go to waste."

"Very good," Stephanie said. She smiled at the four of us and I could see the wheels spinning in her head.

She knows, I thought.

"Oh, big spender," Monica said, mocking me.

"Of course," I answered her and then changed the subject by adding, "The waitress suspects."

Mark nodded. "Maybe it takes one to know one."

"Oh that's hot."

"Boys!" Lea said. "Stop thinking with your dicks." When she said dicks her hand brushed my erection. I jumped.

"You okay dude?" Mark asked.

"Can you ask your wife to keep her hands to herself," I said jokingly.

He looked directly across the table at Lea and said dryly, "Slut."

She smiled. "You don't know the half of it."

"Oh really? Tell me all about your amorous adventures young lady."

She laughed and shook her hair. "Oh we don't have time and I'm sure that our friends don't want to hear them."

"Oh we do," I said.

Monica rolled her eyes at me again. This was twice so far tonight. So far I was on pace for a new record. "Behave," she told me playfully.

"Why?"

I felt Lea's hand on my leg again. Nice.

"You would never believe me," Lea said.

I would. From our conservation at the club last week I knew that Mark and Lea have had more experience than us even though they were fairly new at this. We were relatively old dogs at this game, but hadn't done anything other than swapping wives.

The waitress came with a bottle and a couple of glasses. She pretended not to notice Lea's hand on my leg and whatever was happening on the other side of the table. I suspected that my wife's right hand was touching Mark somehow. My imagination pictured her small hand rubbing his crotch. This made me hard.

"Who will taste the wine?" Stephanie asked.

"I will," I said.

She poured a little in my glass. I took only enough

to cleanse my pallet and then I tasted it. "Hmmm...crushed grapes," I said.

Everyone laughed including the waitress who looked at me for an answer.

"It is good," I told her.

"I am glad that you like our crushed grapes," she said. She looked at me like she was having fun.

"I do," I said.

"Anything else?" She asked the table.

"No, we are good for now," Lea said.

"Okay, enjoy."

Stephanie turned and a hand brushed my cock. I looked at Lea and said, "You are torturing me."

"I know."

We drank and the conversation turned to a topic other than sex. This helped me lose my erection and that was good. I am sure that with Lea around that my erection wasn't too far off. When needed I am positive that it would come back with a vengeance.

I looked around at the patrons of the bar. They looked like a conservative type of crowd. Actually, they looked very boring. They drank and danced without really touching. The music was alright, top forty stuff, but the place looked like it was the last place on Earth to have fun.

I heard my name called. "What?" I asked.

"We should dance," Lea said. She looked at me and then at Monica who said, "Good idea."

The four of us headed for the dance floor and I wasn't sure who was going to dance with whom. All I knew was that I didn't want to dance with Mark. If Mark and I danced together then that would be really too much for this vanilla crowd. It was too much for some swinger clubs; not that I have ever done it or even plan to.

On the dance floor I paired up with Lea and Monica paired up with Mark. We danced a respectable distance apart and even though we didn't give any indication of anything going on the waitress eyed us with interest. Somehow she knew and Mark's statement popped into my head, "Takes one to know one."

The next song was slower so we moved together

and I enjoyed having Lea in my arms. Stephanie and I both noticed that Monica and Mark danced even closer to each other than Lea and I.

Halfway through the song I decided to go for it. I leaned over to kiss Lea and she happily kissed me back. We made out on the dance floor. So did Monica and Mark.

I was positive that our observant waitress saw us and I didn't care. We made out for a few minutes and when we finished nobody in the bar registered any disapproval. In fact, the place was still dull. Maybe if someone would disapprove of our actions it would liven up the place. I looked around and everyone seemed to be half asleep. Nor could I see the waitress.

She is probably in the kitchen, I thought.

At the end of the song, Lea thanked me for the dance and said that she wanted to go back to the table. I told her that I would meet her there after I went to the toilet.

We left Monica and Mark on the dance floor. They had stopped kissing, but their bodies were still pressed together. Hot.

I did my business in the toilet and when I came out

I almost bumped into the waitress. "Sorry," I said to her.

"No problem." She looked at me curiously and then asked, "Can I ask you a question?"

"Sure, what is it?"

"Are you all in the lifestyle?" she asked me quietly.

"Yes, is it obvious?"

"No, but I saw who walked in with who and..."

"Right."

She giggled. "Don't worry your secret is safe with me."

"Thank you."

She made a motion to leave and I said, "Um..."

She stopped and asked, "What is it?"

"Are you?"

She smiled and winked at me.

I watched her cute ass walk towards the bar. My erection was coming back to life. I was half hard by the time I got back to Lea at the table.

"Trying to pick up the waitress," she asked. By her tone she was teasing me.

"No I wasn't. She knows."

"Oh..."

"And she is cool with it. Actually, I am sure that she is in the lifestyle herself."

"Right, takes one to know one."

"Your husband is wise."

We both looked at our spouses on the dance floor and they were making out again.

"They so want to fuck each other," Lea said and that was all my erection needed for it to come back fully.

I leaned over and I kissed Lea. The kiss was long and passionate and I wanted her right there and then.

"Slow down tiger," she said. "We are in a public place."

"I know."

I looked around and as per usual most people were too much into their own business to notice what

Dick Talent

we were doing. I said most people. A couple at the bar were glaring at Lea and I.

"Holy shit," I blurted out loud.

"What is it?"

"That is the sour-faced woman. The legend is true."

"Who?" She looked confused so I told her the story. "Oh that is just great," she said after hearing about this woman. "I hope that you are wrong and that is just someone else."

"Me too!"

The woman started to come our way and her husband followed.

"Oh shit," I said. "Here they come."

"Maybe they are just leaving."

I looked at Lea and the woman stopped at our table. I didn't want to turn to face her so I didn't.

"Hello," she said.

I rolled my eyes at Lea.

"Yes, can we help you?" Lea asked pleasantly.

"God knows what you are doing and he told me for you to stop it," she said.

"Um, what are we doing?" I asked. My tone of

173

voice wasn't nearly as pleasant as Lea's.

"You are fornicating with another man's wife," she said arrogantly.

Lea gasped and I laughed. "But this is my wife," I said.

The man finally said something, "But you walked in with the slut that's on the dance floor."

"Slut? That is rude. You mean Mark's wife? We were out shopping together. Is that a sin?"

The couple glared at me and finally the sour-faced woman said, "No shopping with someone else's wife isn't a sin. But what were you shopping for?"

"A present for Mark, if it is any of your business."

She glared at me for a minute and I went back to my wine. I took a sip and then said to her, "Anything else?"

"I think that you are lying."

"You know what, I don't care, please go away."

I turned back to Lea and smiled at her.

"You can't turn your back on god and get away with it," the sour-faced woman said. "God told me what you have done and he told me. You are an adulterous. You will burn in hell for it."

"Fine. Now fuck off!" I said it so that other people could hear that I was displeased.

Monica and Mark both gazed our way from the dance floor. A couple of dozen of other people were now looking our way. The looks on their faces suggested that this was about as lively as things got in this place.

"Now, you can't talk to my wife like that," the guy told me.

"So she can be as rude to me as she wants, but I can't stick up for myself." I groaned. "Fuck off."

"Yes she can say whatever is necessary. God has given her the right to be the judge and jury. She has the gift."

"Oh my God you are two are so fucked up!"

By now everyone was looking our way.

The bartender came over and I said to him, "Can you please tell these people to stop bothering us?"

"Sir, I am going to ask you to keep your voice down," the bartender said.

"Yes sir I will, as long as these two never speak to me again."

"Sir!" He looked uncomfortable with the situation.

I turned to Lea and asked, "So how is your night going?"

She giggled and shook her head.

"God knows..." the sour-faced woman said, but was cut-off by the bartender who said, "Mary they aren't listening to you. Best to left them be."

I tried to block her protests out of my head by asking Lea what she wants to drink next. To my delight, the bartender somehow convinced the holier than thou couple to move on. By the time that I turned my gaze from Lea, they were out of sight.

"She is gone," Lea said. "Wow, what a mixed up bitch. I can't believe that people like that exist."

"Yes. The legend is true."

Stephanie came to the table and said, "Well done. You got rid of the vortex bitch, she sucks all the pleasure out of here."

Monica and Mark came to the table.

"Who the hell was that?" Mark asked.

Stephanie explained it to them and it matched

what I knew and then added, "She acts like she owns the place and anyone with any sense of fun never comes back here. She makes sure of that. I hope that you guys come back. You guys are fun."

We thanked her and it looked like she had something more to say, but didn't know how to say it.

"What is on your mind?" Monica asked her.

"Can I join you?"

"Sure," Mark said and I said in unison.

"Have you had any experience?" Monica asked.

Quietly she said, "My ex-boyfriend and I were part of the lifestyle for a few years and seeing you four flirt with each other has brought back a lot of good memories."

I nodded. "What time do you get off?"

* * * * *

To my disbelief an hour later the five of us entered Mark and Lea's condo.

"Help me with drinks," Mark asked me and I went with him as the women sat on the chesterfield. The bar was within sight of the chesterfield so we could see the women talk. He whispered to me, "Let them do their thing."

Stephanie sat in the middle of the three women and was also the center of attention. Monica's right hand caressed her leg as Lea played with her hair.

They are going to make-out, I thought.

Sure enough Lea and Stephanie kissed.

"That didn't take long," Mark said.

Next, Monica kissed Stephanie and then afterwards kissed Lea. The three of them took turns making out with each other and I was hard. I was fucking rock hard.

Mark and I abandoned the drinks and came behind our wives. He spooned Monica while I sat behind Lea's wonderful body.

Stephanie's blouse was undone and her white bra was showing. As Monica and Lea kissed she said to me, "I haven't been laid in so long." She looked hungrily at me and I smiled. I swear I lost of bit of cum right there and then.

I leaned behind Lea and found the young woman's lips. Her lips were soft and her tongue was busy.

She was clearly in heat. After enjoying the kiss I repositioned myself in front of Lea and Stephanie. I had a hard decision to make. Who to go down on first? And how do I not offend one of them? Oh, the etiquette of the lifestyle. Then it hit me: Lea should be first. Stephanie, as lovely as she was, was a bonus to this party.

I spread Lea's legs and she smiled. I winked at Stephanie and said, "You're next."

She licked her lips and she started to undress. Actually, everyone was busy taking their clothes off. I was last to the party. I pulled off my shirt and undid my pants as I leaned in to kiss Lea between her legs.

Clean shaven my tongue attacked her lips. She moaned and I spread her lips. I heard my wife moan and looked up to see that Mark's head was between her legs. Stephanie was busy too. She nuzzled Lea's neck and played with her tits with her hands. Her ass was more or less in my face. Nice. I reached up, licked my fingers and then gently played with Stephanie pussy as my face went back into Lea's pussy. I heard both women moan. This was too much fun.

Monica moaned next and I was glad that she was

enjoying herself. Get off baby, I thought. Get your rocks off.

"Allow me," Mark said to me.

"Sure."

His fingers replaced mine in Stephanie's pussy and the third woman became sort of a time share. Next Monica fingered her and Stephanie moaned, "It has been too long."

As this was going on I concentrated on Lea's clit and judging by the way she was squirming I knew that she was close to cumming. I heard a woman have an orgasm, but it was my wife not Lea. Stephanie stopped panting because Monica was too busy cumming to fuck her with her fingers.

I intensified my efforts attacking Lea's clit until she was next. By the time she had stopped cumming in my face the other three had shifted positions. Stephanie was on her back with my wife's face between her legs while Mark fucked Monica doggie-style.

Time to fuck, I thought.

Mark thought so too. He tossed me a condom and I put it on. Lea smiled at me with her legs wide open. Finally, the erection that I've had for most of the night was going to the place that it wanted to. I slid into Lea's pussy and moaned. Very nice.

Somehow Stephanie managed to get her head under Lea so she could lick her pussy. Again, very nice.

But she didn't stop there; something was lightly touching my balls.

It must be the waitress, I thought.

I haven't had too much experience with my balls being licked, but I knew that Stephanie was doing a good job. She had done this before.

I watched Stephanie's body squirm with pleasure. The young woman was going nuts. She couldn't get enough sex.

"We've unleashed a sex demon," Mark said watching her.

"Yes," was all I could say back to him.

I watched my wife's tongue lick the waitress' pussy and together with the pleasure I felt with Lea's pussy squeezing my cock and the tongue on my balls, I surrendered to pleasure; cum flew out of my cock and I groaned as load after load escaped my body.

I fell backwards and landed on the carpet. I was out of action, but the action didn't stop. Stephanie's next victim was Lea who was only too willing to be eaten by her.

Oh my god, I thought. This waitress has been working in a vanilla bar and suffering for too long. She is a wild one hidden in a tame prison. She must have felt like she was undercover.

I was happy that we had freed a fellow undercover swinger.

As I watched four naked people help each other get off, I felt my cock slowly come back to life. I smiled because I knew exactly who I was going to fuck next.

Dick Talent

Sex Club Romance

"Big cocks are a lot of fun, but they can hurt."

I looked at the woman who just said this to me as
we danced and I pictured her with a big cock in her
mouth. She looked like a cocksucker. Um, I mean
that in a good way. She was pretty and busty, two
things that I liked in a woman. Her hair was chestnut brown and long.

I continued to dance and Paula continued, "Give
me a normal size cock with an owner who knows
how to use it."

"Okay, I am your man," I said to her and then
smiled. I looked around the club. It was busy, but
most of the clients were men or couples. Paula was
one of the few single women. This was a typical
Friday night at a swingers club and over the last
few months I had learned to accept the fact that the
odds were never in my favor. Tonight I was happy
just to be dancing with a hot woman.

She smiled back, but also gave me a look that I de-
duced as: you are a single man at a sex club, you
are a dime a dozen so be good or I'll move onto the
next guy. This was reinforced when she said, "You

183

men are always in a rush to jump into bed with any woman. Slow down. I need to get to know you first."

I told myself to be cool and I might just get my dick wet tonight. So, I just nodded and didn't challenge her statement. I just said, "Right" and continued to dance.

We finished the song and then we went over to the side of the dance floor to talk. This was her idea. I was happy that I still had her attention and that she hadn't moved onto some other guy. I knew that I wasn't the best looking guy in the club tonight. I am pretty confident that I was above average in looks, but I am no model.

"So tell me about yourself," she said. She looked at me and she seemed generally interested.

I knew that I had to be interesting so I didn't know what to say. "What do you want to know?"

Of course whenever you have something someone else is always too willing to try to take it away from you so I wasn't surprised that a guy interrupted our conversation. He reeked of overconfidence or was it just his cologne? I don't know, I hated him instantly and I wanted him to go away.

Then again, who wouldn't hate him when he was moving in on your turf?

The guy was so pushy that he half blocked me by standing right in front of me. I fought the urge to punch this guy in the ribs. "You are a fine looking woman," he said to Paula and ignored me. "What is your name?"

"Not interested," she said. "And if you excuse us we were in the middle of a conversation."

The pushy guy looked over his shoulder at me and muttered, "What, with him?" And then he scuffed.

"Nice," I said under my breath. I really wanted to hit the little twerp now.

He didn't move out of the way so Paula took a step to the left and I did the same. We were now face to face and I smirked.

"So you were just about to tell me about yourself before we were rudely interrupted." She stared directly at me, ignoring the other guy.

Finally the guy went away, but not before saying, "You are settling for second best."

"Thank you for that," I said to Paula.

"No problem. I've had a lot of practice with pushy jerks. It is the hazard of being here on nights where single men are allowed. Men are pushy enough when they are with their wives."

"Single male here so this is the only night that I am allowed in the club, so I am happy that you are here braving the riff-raft."

"You are single. You are not married or have a girl-friend?" She looked at me right in the eye and I could tell that she was serious. I sensed that she had met a few guys here that claimed to be single and weren't.

"Never been married and I am not seeing anyone right now." She smiled and I continued, "I've been single for six months. My ex - and this will be the only time that I will ever talk about her - broke up and it wasn't good. I never ever want to see her again. She is a..." I stopped before I called her something that I shouldn't. "Sorry."

"How long were you two together?"

"Four, four and a half years."

"Why did you two break up?"

I decided to be perfectly honest. "Sex. I love it and she wanted it less and less to the point where it only happened once a month, if that."

She gasped. "Who can live on that? My last relationship was like that only I was the one who wanted it more. We broke up when he caught me masturbating."

The image of her masturbating was very pleasing to the imagination. "Why would he get mad at that? I would love to walk in on a girlfriend who was playing with herself."

She giggled. "Well, I had another man's cock in my mouth at the time." She had a devious look on her face and then giggled again.

"Oh that would do it. Bad girl," I said playfully. I found her story to be hot. This woman liked sex. And since I liked woman who liked sex, I liked this woman.

She picked up on that. "So what would have you done in that situation?"

"Probably join in."

She giggled. "Really?"

I nodded and smiled. I was getting hard and her cute little giggle added to it. She sounded so playful every time that she giggled.

"Really."

"You wouldn't be jealous? My ex was so jealous all the time."

I winked at her. "I was always taught to share."

I could tell that she liked that and she looked at me like she was contemplating dropping to her knees and blowing me right then and there. I know I would like that.

"Okay," she said. "We both really like sex and are into having multiple partners. We have that in common. I think that most people here have that in common. What else do we have in common?"

For the next hour we talked about family, friends and hobbies. She allowed me to buy her a couple of drinks and she fought off a couple more attempts by pushy guys.

"Can't you see that I'm in deep negotiations here?" She asked one guy.

"With him? Sorry I thought that he was your husband. You two have been talking for a long time."

He went away and I said, "Well, at least he was nice about it."

She stared at me. "Yes, he did; husband." She giggled and I laughed. I actually didn't mind the thought of being her husband. My wife has a great rack and likes to swing, I thought. Sounds good to me.

She looked over at the guy who was just here and licked her lips. "Actually he is kind of cute. If we were married would you let me get it on with him?"

"Can I join in or at least watch?"

"Of course."

I nodded.

We locked eyes and I felt the chemistry between us. I wanted her and she acted like she wanted me.

"At the risk of being pushy," I said, "May I kiss you?"

"Yes. I have been waiting for you to ask for a while now."

I moved close to her, put my hands on her waist and looked down. She looked up expectantly and looked beautiful. I leaned down and her lips met my lips halfway. Her lips were perfect as I slid my lips against hers. Her tongue was the first to explore. It parted my lips.

Aggressive, I thought, sexually aggressive. I like that in a woman.

My tongue intercepted her tongue and she moaned softy. I also felt her oversized chest against my chest. Bib boobs were pressing against me. I was hard.

After a few minutes, she broke it off and said, "Nice."

"Very nice."

She hugged me and whispered in my ear. "Fuck me."

"Where?"

"My place. Follow me."

"Okay."

It felt great walking out with Paula because I knew that most of the guys who tried to pick her up saw us leaving together. Even if nothing happened after we left I still won in my eyes.

Her place was a nice condo in the suburbs. I complimented her on her hiring the right interior decorator. They did a great job.

"I did it myself," she said proudly.

"I'm impressed."

She stood in front of me and looked up. "I like tall men."

"I like pretty women."

"I do too, but we can talk about that later."

"Oh." This woman's great attitude towards sex was blowing my mind.

She giggled. "Did that make you hard?" she cupped the bulge in my pants. "Yep. You are hard."

I moaned.

"Want to spend the night?"

"Yes."

"Promise me one thing."

"What?"

"That this isn't just a one night stand."

"I promise."

"And you are not married or anything?"

"There is no one waiting for me so I can spend the night with you without anyone getting mad at me."

She quickly dropped to her knees and undid my belt. The zipper was next and my pants came down. Next my underwear was lowered and she came eye to eye with my cock.

"Fuck you're big," she said.

"I'm not that long."

"No, you're really thick. Big."

"Oh, is that a problem."

"Remember what I said about big cocks are fun, but can hurt."

"I'll be as gentle as I can."

She nodded and dropped to her knees. It blows my mind seeing a good looking woman engulf a cock in her mouth. My cock disappeared into Paula's pretty mouth and my cock jumped. I was as hard as I could be. She said that I was really big, but she got all of my cock in her mouth. Experience I guess.

I moaned. Yes, she was experienced. She knew that she was doing. Oh god, she really knew what she was doing. I was so close to cumming that her skills were torture. I concentrated on not cumming. Anyhow I am pretty sure that she got a taste of per-cum.

She stopped and I stood motionless with my eyes closed.

"Are you okay?" She asked.

"I was just about to cum."

"I know. That's why I stopped." She giggled. "Aren't you going to watch me undress?"

I opened my eyes and saw a great pair of tits in a white bra. She undid the bra and I licked my lips at the sight of her naked tits. Her large tits hung heavily and I don't think that I saw anything as beautiful.

"Do you like?" She asked.

I stared at them and started to jerk myself.

She slid off her panties. I didn't answer as I watched her fall on her back and spread her legs. Her pussy hair was neatly kept and actually matched her hair color. It was chestnut brown. I gently spread her pussy lips apart with my fingers and inserted my tongue in between them. I worked my way to her clit as she squirmed.

"Yep," she reported over and over again every ten seconds or so. This intensified and became more frequent as she got closer to having an orgasm. "Yep........yep.......yep.....yep..."

I attacked the clit relentlessly.

"Yep! Yep!" She arched her back and moaned loudly. She had her first orgasm of our relation-ship. I hoped to hear her have many many more big O's.

My turn. My condom covered cock slid into her well lubed pussy and she wrapped all four of her limbs around me. "Fuck your big!"

"Does it hurt?"

"No. It feels wonderful. Perfect size. Fuck me."

I am sure that she was over-stating my size for my benefit, but I didn't care. It was damn hot and good for my ego. It also made me hump her hard and faster.

She bit my shoulder. It wasn't hard and it was actually cute the way she did it.

This woman is passionate, I thought. She is beautiful, passionate and hornier than a rabbit. Perfect.

She arched her back and I looked down at her huge tits. That did it. I came hard and bucked her madly until every drop left my cock. Then I collapsed beside her.

"God that was good," I said. "You were wonderful."

"Okay, we got the sex part covered," she said and then giggled.

I got up and she asked me where I was going. She sounded worried.

"To the washroom to get rid of the condom."

"Oh, right."

I came back and pulled the covers up as I lay on my back. She turned off the light and cuddled into me. She giggled.

"What is so funny?" I asked.

"Who would have thought that I would find a boyfriend in a sex club."

I liked being referred to as her boyfriend. I also liked her before having sex with her and I really liked her after fucking her brains out. "Yes," I said, "It is the start of the great sex club romance."

She giggled again.

First Time Orgy

We all love sex, but how many people engage or would ever consider participating in an orgy? I never thought I would. Imagine being naked with a roomful of strangers who are all touching each other? It was strange enough just being naked with my wife and two other people at the same time. It was also damn sexy hot and we have slept with a few other couples with varied results since. Some were hot and some were just alright. Even the just alright was still good. As they say, even bad sex is good. Well, for a guy at least.

Of course the first couple of times I had problems getting and keeping an erection. Don't laugh or criticize until you have been there. There is tremendous pressure on guys to perform. I say, I have a whole new respect for male porn stars. It isn't easy. You think that it would be a no brainer with a couple of naked women who are all ready to go. I guess that I am not superman and the first time I made the mistake of thinking about it too much.

Anyhow by the third time swapping I had gotten used to the unusual situation and relaxed and enjoyed the experience. Of course the more that I relaxed the harder I was and the harder I was the more the women liked it. So, in short, at this stage Anne and I were experienced swingers who were looking for other hot couples to play with. Yes, I'm still very attracted to my wife but after nine years of marriage I am finding myself flirting with other women.

Anne has long black hair, green eyes, high cheek bones and a body like a fashion model. Her legs are long and shapely, her ass small and perfectly round and her breasts are perky. She doesn't look like an accountant and certainly doesn't act like one. Get a couple of drinks into her and she forgets about everything and has a good time. Needless to say we enjoyed a very good sex life. Well, I think it is a good sex life and if you had a chance to get it on with someone who looked like Anne, you would think that it was a good sex life too.

The third Saturday night in the mouth was our usual time to go to the club and this Saturday was no exception. Tonight was our adult play night. Lord knows I have been looking forward to this since the last time. Driving home I was already thinking about the next time.

The club is buried in an industrial park and if you weren't looking for it, you would never know it was there. Or if you happen to spot it you would think that it was just a normal dance club, which isn't too far from the truth. The club is pretty much a normal dance club, but the big difference is that they have an area in the back with beds, lockers and private rooms. Towels and condoms are provided. We've gone to the back a few times with other couples and have always found a private room with a bed in it. Still, it didn't stop everyone from pulling back the curtains, but it did keep out the majority of people.

Anyhow, I wonder what tonight would bring. As part of our routine, once we were in, we got a drink at the bar and then spoke to people that we've met before. I didn't mind this because it always took Anne a few drinks to get her onto the dance floor and the dance floor was where the action began.

The dance floor was busy, but we found an empty spot by the cage. We danced a few feet apart and I looked around. Two couples were into each other close by and I wanted to be part of it. However, I knew that I had to respect the fact that they were hooking up with each other.

One couple was hot and I knew that Anne would like the guy. He was her type, tall, lean and handsome. She was cute. Her pleasant figure looked good in the tan pants and flowered blouse. She dressed like she could go to church wearing what she was wearing and it gave me the impression that they were newbies.

The other woman was a complete opposite of the cutie. She had pure white hair and an attitude towards sex that was anything but pure. She was a wild one and I was glad that she grinded into Anne.

Her man wore thick glasses wasn't shy about things. He came behind Anne and pushed his crotch into her backside.

Bubbles is horny, I joked to myself.

If you don't know Bubbles is a character on a show called, The Trailer Park Boys. This guy reminded me of him and I couldn't see Anne being into him. The other guy yes, but not him. Speaking of which the other guy the tall, thin and handsome guy noticed Anne checking him out. His wife, the little cutie backed into me. I did not mind.

Somehow we became part of their foursome, which made me happy. I heard Anne, Stuart and Bev, exchange names.

So here was the situation. Bubbles was behind Anne and his hands were playing with her tits.

Stuart was with Bubble's woman, Bev. I looked at her, she was a curvy woman with a guy's attitude towards sex. They were face to face and I wondered when they were going to kiss. I wondered when I was going to kiss...um, what is her name? Hang on.

"What's your name?" I whispered into the cutie's ear.

"Lisa."

"Lisa, you are one good looking woman."

She turned her head and kissed me on the lips. It seemed that she was into me. Hurrah.

It looks like I am going to dip my cock into new territory tonight, I thought.

I looked at Anne. That's if Anne gave the green light of course. And right now I don't think that she will. Bubbles was on her and I could tell that she liked the attention, but not really who was giving it to her. I quietly rooted for the other guy to take over. And if he did, maybe the other two would go away so Anne and I could have cutie and handsome boy to ourselves.

"What is your husband's name?" I asked Lisa.

"Stuart."

All three women forced each other in a triangle and hugged each other. It was hot. Boobs rubbed against boobs and nipples poked through blouses. Bev was the leader of the sluts and she pulled Anne even closer to her and kissed her deeply.

Nice, but wrong couple, I thought.

Bev kissed Lisa next. Sweet. There was a moment right after that Anne and Lisa stood and just looked at each other. Neither one of them wanted to make the first move.

"Come on you two," Bev said and with each hand pushed the two women closer to each other. "Kiss."

Yes Bev! My cock grew harder watching two pretty women tenderly kiss each other. It wasn't a long kiss, but it was nice.

The three guys each had a woman. I had Bev, Stuart held Anne and Bubbles had Lisa. I wanted to switch things up, but I could wait to see if it happened naturally. However, the more time that I spent with Bev the more that I liked her. Her attitude towards sex was awesome. I felt that she wanted to strip and get it on right here on the dance floor.

All six of us grinded each other for a few songs more and then it happened. We all overheated.

"God it's hot. I need a drink," Bev said.

"Me too," Anne said.

The three men were sent to the bar for drinks as the women found seats. We came back and I remained silent as the six of us drank. The other four seemed to have agreed with each other that they were going to fuck in the back right after their drinks. Of course I wanted to be part of it.

Bev asked Anne and I, "Do you guys want to come to the back with us?"

Anne surprised me when she said, "Yes."

Bev smiled at me. "Great! Let's go."

The four of them started towards the back and I asked Anne, "We don't have to do this."

"I want to. Looks like fun. Are you good with this?"

"Yes. Let's do it."

We headed for the back and at the counter I grabbed a lock and a couple of towels. We found a locker that wasn't too close to the other two couples. I didn't want to change in front of them. I actually force myself not to watch the other women as they strip. I want to see them naked for the first time while we are in bed and not before. It sort of ruins it when I see them changing.

Anne and I put our clothes into the same locker and I wrapped the chord for the key around my wrist so I wouldn't lose it. With only towels on we found and followed the other two couples as they walked into the play area. As we got close I heard the sounds of moans and the occasional slap. People were fucking and it was busy here tonight. It was too busy because all of the private rooms were filled. Damn.

"Where to?" Bev asked.

In the middle of the play area were a couple of empty beds. One was a large bed that was raised about three feet above the floor. It was high. I had to help Anne climb on top of it. Stuart followed her and helped her out of her towel. What a gentleman! They kissed and I got onto the bed. I felt exposed and I looked around. Four private rooms were on one side and four were on the other side.

All of the rooms were full with at least one couple inside of them. Only about half of them had the curtains closed so I could see people fucking. In one I watched two women in a sixty-nine as their husbands watched as they jerked themselves off.

I reminded myself that I wasn't here only to watch. I was here for to be part of the action. I looked at Lisa and she fell naked into my arms so I kissed her. It quickly progressed. Lisa looked lovely in the doggy position and I humped her as I admired the view. To my right Stuart was on top of Anne kissing her. They kissed for the longest time and I knew what was going on. Stuart had troubles getting hard so Anne was getting bored. She reached over and played with Lisa's pussy as I fucked her. The little cutie was being double teamed and since I couldn't see her face I wondered if she was enjoying this.

I asked Anne, "Do you think she is enjoying this?"

We both heard Lisa say, "Yes," as she moaned.

I increased my speed and hung on. I wanted to see Lisa have an orgasm and judging by the way that Anne was working her clit I knew that it wouldn't be long before she did.

Bev and Bubbles were fucking on the floor just to my left. I smiled at her and she smiled back. "You're next," I whispered.

"Alright," she yelped.

Lisa bucked and squirmed and I was surprised how quiet she was when she came. Some women are quiet I told myself. Anne is very quiet when she cums. Actually, it is about the only time that she is quiet. Usually she is rambling on about something.

Anyhow, I pulled out when I thought that Lisa was done. Anne's hand was already gone. She knew that we had gotten Lisa off before I did.

Bubbles came over and said to me, "My turn." He sounded a little impatient and annoyed. I didn't care. That was his problem.

"Sure."

I smiled at Bev who was sitting on a bed that was adjoined to the high bed that I was on. It was lower by half the distance to the ground.

"Your bed or mine?" Bev asked.

I laughed and I stepped down onto her bed. "Hello," I said just before I kissed her.

"New condom," she said.

I looked down and the outside of the condom I was wearing was covered with Lisa liquid. Bev happily exchanged condoms and gave me a nice little hummer to boot. What a nice woman.

"Let me do you," I said to her.

"No Brian ate me already. Fuck me. I'm ready."

She spread and I slid into new territory. It was the second new pussy tonight. Damn! Life is good.

As we fucked a couple came onto the bed and was too close for my comfort for a couple of reasons. Part of it was that they weren't invited, but mostly because I wasn't attracted to them; him especially because I'm straight, but I was not attracted to her because she was too large. Not my type. I don't mind curvy women, but this woman was so large that she didn't have any curves. Her figure was straight from her boobs to the hips. Yuck, not attractive to me. Still, more power to her for coming out and empowering her sexuality.

Bev has a few extra pounds and I don't mind. On her they looked good. She is sexy.

Bev was thinking the same thing when she said to me, "We should move."

"Yes."

Bev got down on all fours on the high bed facing away from the heavy couple and smiled at me. I entered her and moaned. Tight and wet and her curves looked great from this angle. God I love swinging!

I looked over to my right and Anne was in the same position, but she had a different guy on top of her. I glanced down as Brian entered her and thought my god Bubbles was hung. He slid it into her and I could tell it was a tight fit. I was a little jealous, but I was really turned on by the situation. If I was a woman I would get off by a big dick. I know, what a guy's way of thinking. Anyhow, he pounded Anne with his big dick and she looked like she was loving it. If I know Anne she probably was loving being stretched.

Slut, I thought and smiled. My wife is such a slut. I sighed. Fuck that turned me on.

Meanwhile I fucked Bev doggy style and I couldn't help looking around. As I just had mentioned, my wife was to our right getting fucked by Bubbles and Lisa and Stuart were kissing in front of us. They were both standing and he looked like he was still having erectile dysfunction. I felt sorry for him. Been there, done that.

I pulled out of Bev, saw my rock hard dick and rammed it back in. Bev moaned.

"God, this is the most fun that I've ever had here," she said to me.

"Really?"

"Yes. Let's switch positions."

"Okay."

I pulled out and watched her move onto her back.

"This is my last time here. I have a boyfriend now." I looked at Bubbles. "No, Brian is just my fuck buddy and this is our last time together. The next time that you see him here he will be with another girl. I won't be back."

"Oh that is too bad." I was disappointed. I liked Bev. She had the perfect combination of looks and passion, which I didn't appreciate when I first met her.

"Maybe I can get the new boyfriend into swinging."

I smiled. "That would be good."

"But he is pretty straight laced." He actually likes

going to church."

"Church?"

"Yes," she said nodding and giggling. "He is a real goodie-goodie."

"Too bad."

"So…" she smiled at me.

I reinserted my cock into her wet pussy. I was determined to give her the time of her life. I made sure that every thrust was hard and strong. She seemed to like what I was doing. I noticed that Lisa's legs were now by Bev's head and since I was taller than her I could kiss her legs as I fucked Bev. She spread her legs and looked right at me with lust in her eyes. Somehow I got harder than I had been, which I didn't think was possible. Lisa helped by moving her pussy to within licking distance. Hmmm…I can take a hint.

I humped Bev as I ate Lisa's pussy. This was my first time pleasing two women at the same time. Bev saw what I was doing and laughed. "You are a stud."

She grabbed my ass and squeezed. "Faster!"

Stuart kneelt by Lisa's head and she grabbed his limp cock.

The familiar touch of your wife should really help matters, I thought.

It did. Stuart got hard and Lisa sucked him in unison to my pussy licking. I felt a connection between her and I. Unfortunately it was broken when he came and pushed his cock out of her mouth. The part of his load that didn't land in her mouth landed on her face and she acted like she didn't like it. She didn't. To my disappointment she left immediately to get cleaned up. Anne and Brian left too. Apparently they were also done.

"Just us," I said.

She smiled.

I leaned down and tenderly kissed her. She whimpered. I increased my speed and shifted my weight to my arms so that I could see her better. I looked at her big round tits bouncing with each thrust. Nice.

"Oh, here we go," I said just before cum started to leave my body.

"Thank you for a great time. This was the most fun

that I've ever had back here."

I nodded. "Me too."

"Yeah, right." She giggled.

"The was my first orgy and I couldn't have picked two better women to share it with."

"Aw, you're sweet."

The others came back with a bottle of water each. Anne handed one to me.

"Thanks."

Stuart, Lisa and Anne sat on the bed and talked. Bubbles sat on an empty bed with his dick in the air. Really he did. He had a boner and he looked like he was waiting for someone to take care of it for him and something told me that he wasn't too fussy who it was. Um, no thanks.

I finished the water and Anne noticed. "We should go," she said. "Let's say goodbye to everyone."

"Right."

In the car I asked Anne what she thought of our first orgy and she smiled. "It was fun even with Stuart not being able to get it up."

"Newbie."

"Yeah, I hate newbies."

"You prefer Brian and his big dick. I didn't think that he was your type."

"Some of it was good. The actual fucking felt nice." She groaned. "I hope that you are satisfied for a while because I am going to be sore tomorrow. I might be out of action for a bit."

I smiled and thought of Lisa and Bev, my two cuties on one night. "Don't worry; I'm good...for now."

About the Author

Dick Talent has written several novels and short stories on the lighter side of love and sex. His first story, *"So Close Yet So Far"* was first published in 2011 and is included in his short story collection, *"Getting Some "Tale"*.

"Village Bicycle" is a story about a young woman who is stuck working for her parents and the bicycle she takes to work every day isn't the only thing that gets ridden.

"Four Play" is a story of a man who talks his wife into swinging and enjoys watching her lose herself in passion.

"The Penetrator" is about a fireman who has an oversized hose and thinks that his purpose in life is to put out women's fires. He enjoys it, women enjoy it, but his wife doesn't. She is determined to keep him at home and under her control.

"First Time Orgy" is the prelude to "Swinging at a Vanilla Resort".

Blue Ops Pocket

Books:

Kelly's Wild Side by Rachel Richards

Into the Swing by Rachel Richards

A Swinging Couple by Rachel Richards

Swinger Sex Games by Rachel Richards

Becoming Bisexual* by Rachel Richards

Four on the Bed* by Rachel Richards and Aaron Knight

Unusual Stories of Lust and Power by Dick Talent

Swinging by Dick Talent

Promiscuous People* by Dick Talent

Coming Out Confessions* by Neil Downe

AC/DCs* by Neil Downe

* coming soon

Blue Ops EBooks

#	Title	Author(s)	Release Date
1	Kelly's Wild Side (originally called She's in Control)	Rachel Richards	Aug. 2011
2	So Close, Yet So Far	Dick Talent	Aug. 2011
3	Getting Some "Tale"	Dick Talent	Sept. 2011
4	Village Bicycle	Dick Talent	Sept. 2011
5	University Days (excerpt from Kelly's Wide Side)	Rachel Richards	Sept. 2011
6	Confessions of a Bisexual Man Part I: The Beginning	Neil Downe	Oct. 2011
7	Into the Swing	Rachel Richards	Oct. 2011
8	Confessions of a Bisexual Man Part II: On the Down Low	Neil Downe	Oct. 2011
9	Confessions of a Bisexual Man Part III: Second Dates	Neil Downe	Oct. 2011
10	Confessions of a Bisexual Man Part IV: Best of Both Worlds	Neil Downe	Oct. 2011
11	Confessions of a Bisexual Man (I to IV)	Neil Downe	Nov. 2011
12	House Guest	Neil Downe	Nov. 2011
13	3 Ways to Happiness	Rachel Richards	Nov. 2011
14	Four Play	Dick Talent	Feb. 2012
15	Bi Curious George	Neil Downe	June 2012
16	Office Confessions	Neil Downe	July 2012
17	50 Shades of Gay	Rachel Richards	Sept. 2012
18	Full Swing	Rachel Richards	Sept. 2012
19	50 Shades of Gay 2	Rachel Richards	Feb. 2013
20	Swinger Sex Games 1: Spin the Bottle	Rachel Richards	Feb. 2013

#	Title	Author(s)	Release Date
21	The Penetrator Part 1: The Fireman	Dick Talent	Feb. 2013
22	Swinger Sex Games 2: A Paradise	Rachel Richards	Feb. 2013
23	Swinger Sex Games 3: Musical Closets	Rachel Richards	March 2013
24	Swinger Sex Games 4: Blindfolds	Rachel Richards	April 2013
25	Sexual Situations	Aaron Knight	June 2013
26	Swinger Sex Games 5: Bondage	Rachel Richards	June 2013
27	Bisexual George	Neil Downe	Aug. 2013
28	The Shower Assistant	Dick Talent	Sept. 2013
29	Bi George	Neil Downe	Sept. 2013
30	Swinger Sex Games 6: Mary's Revenge	Rachel Richards	Oct. 2013
31	Swinger Sex Games (parts 1 to 6)	Rachel Richards	Oct. 2013
32	More 50 Shades of Gay	Rachel Richards	Jan. 2014
33	Slut Wife	Rachel Richards Aaron Knight	Jan. 2014
34	A Sex Church	Rachel Richards Aaron Knight	Jan. 2014
35	Bisexual Swingers	Neil Downe	Feb. 2014
36	Confessions of a Gym Teacher	Rachel Richards	March 2014
37	Penetrator II: The To Do List	Dick Talent	March 2014
38	Into the Swing (second edition)	Rachel Richards	April 2014
39	Swinging Vacation	Dick Talent	May 2014
40	Switching Teams	Rachel Richards	May 2014
41	Penetrator III: A Player to be Named Later	Dick Talent	May 2014
42	Orgy Club	Rachel Richards	May 2014

#	Title	Author(s)	Release Date
43	Penetrator IV: Sex Agent	Dick Talent	June 2014
44	The Penetrator	Dick Talent	June 2014
45	Swinger Sex Games 7: Team Pool	Rachel Richards	Sept. 2014
46	The Best of Bi	Rachel Richards Neil Downe	Sept. 2014
47	Stories of Big O's	Rachel Richards	Sept. 2014
48	Closet Bisexuals	Neil Downe	Oct. 2014
49	Into the Swing II/III (Part II Full Swing & Part III Orgy)	Rachel Richards	Oct. 2014
50	Coming Between Us	Neil Downe	Jan. 2015
51	Party Girl	Rachel Richards Neil Downe	Jan. 2015
52	Overwhelmed by Lust	Rachel Richards	Feb. 2015
53	Wife and Boyfriend Makes Three	Neil Downe	Feb. 2015
54	Learning to Swing	Rachel Richards	Feb. 2015
55	I Married a Nympho	Dick Talent	April 2015
56	Short Stories of Long Men	Neil Downe	May 2015
57	Uncontrollable Lust	Rachel Richards Neil Downe	May 2015
58	First Time Orgy	Dick Talent	May 2015
59	Swinging at the Vanilla Resort	Dick Talent	Aug. 2015
60	My Boyfriend's Boyfriend	Rachel Richards	June 2015
61	Finding Bi Boys	Neil Downe	July 2015
62	Double Teamed	Dick Talent	Oct. 2015
63	Swinger Sex Games 8: Black Friday	Rachel Richards	Nov. 2015
64	(story not published)		
65	Swinger Sex Games 9: Sexual Roulette	Rachel Richards	June 2016
66	Bisexual	Neil Downe	Nov. 2015

#	Title	Author(s)	Release Date
67	Swinger Sex Games 10: Blind Dates	Rachel Richards	Dec. 15
68	Swinging on Vacation	Dick Talent	Dec. 2015
69	Horny People	Dick Talent	Dec. 2015
70	Bi Babes Part I: Liz	Rachel Richards	Dec. 2015
71	Her 1st Sexual Adventure	Rachel Richards	Feb. 2016
72	Her 2nd Sexual Adventure	Rachel Richards	March 2016
73	Her 3rd Sexual Adventure	Rachel Richards	March 2016
74	Her Sexual Adventures	Rachel Richards	March 2016
75	Our 1st Sexual Adventure	Rachel Richards	March 2016
76	Our 2nd Sexual Adventure	Rachel Richards	April 2016
77	Our 3rd Sexual Adventure	Rachel Richards	April 2016
78	Our Sexual Adventures	Rachel Richards	April 2016
79	Becoming a Swinger	Rachel Richards	April 2016
80	Bi Babes II: Strap-on Sally	Rachel Richards	May 2016
81	Three Pillows	Neil Downe	May 2016
82	Undercover Swingers	Dick Talent	May 2016
83	Swingers Part I: Sex Club Romance	Dick Talent	June 2016
84	She Likes Them Bi	Neil Downe	June 2016
85	Hot Tub Playmates	Aaron Knight	May 2016
86	Key Party	Aaron Knight	June 2016
87	Orgy	Aaron Knight	June 2016
88	Swinger Sex Games Box Set 1-10	Rachel Richards	June 2016
89	Swinging (Hot Tub Playmates/Key Party/Orgy)	Aaron Knight	June 2016

#	Title	Author(s)	Release Date
90	Bisexual Sex Party	Neil Downe	June 2016
91	Robin's Lesbian Lovers	Aaron Knight	July 2016

What is next? Find out at: http://jonr29.wix.com/blue-ops